ACCOLADES FOR THE
ALDO ZELNICK COMIC NOVEL SERIES

An alphabetical series for middle-grade readers 7 to 13

2009 Book of the Year Award, juvenile fiction, *ForeWord Reviews*

2010 Colorado Book Award, juvenile literature

2010 Mountains & Plains Independent Booksellers
Association Regional Book Award

2010 *Creative Child* magazine Seal of Excellence

2010 Next Generation Indie Book Award finalist

Winter 2010 Kids' Next Indiebound selection

2011 CYBIL nomination

2011 Independent Publisher Silver "IPPY" Award

2011 *Creative Child* magazine Preferred Choice Award

2012 Texas Bluebonnet Award nomination

WHAT READERS ARE SAYING:

(kid comments are in Aldo's handwriting)

"It was the funniest book I have ever read. The illustrations are hilarious. It is better than Diary of a Wimpy Kid."

- Tavis

"Greg Heffley and Ellie McDoodle, move over—Aldo Zelnick is here!"

— Mary Lee Hahn, teacher and readingyear.blogspot.com blogger

"You will laugh out loud—I guarantee it. The books are THAT funny."

— Becky Bilby, inthepages.blogspot.com

"This is a book that definitely speaks 'kid speak.' The first installment in an A-to-Z Series, *Artsy-Fartsy* is perfect for reluctant readers. It's fun for kids and will be appreciated by parents and teachers for the amusing 'back door' approach to enriching vocabulary. Look out Wimpy Kid!"

— Stacy Morris, Katy Budget Books, Houston, TX

"I REALLY LIKED YOUR ARTSY-FARTSY BOOK. I WOULD PUT IT ON MY TOP 10 LIST."

- Zach

"The other night I caught my 8-year-old twins giggling on the living room couch as they took turns reading *Artsy-Fartsy* aloud to each other. Then one morning I found it on their nightstand with a headlamp resting on the cover from the previous night's under-cover reading. That's a true badge of honor in this house. You hit this one out of the park."

- Becky Jensen

"We talk about the book Bogus at school because it is so cool. I really like it."
- Yisel

One of the most remarkable things about these books is the voice of Aldo, which rings true from every page. The hilarious drawings enhance the text with jokes and visual humor that make Aldo's personality pop.
— Rebecca McGregor, Picture Literacy

"THE BOOK WAS VERY HILARIOUS. IT MADE US LAUGH OUT LOUD. YOU HAVE THE BEST CHARACTERS EVER!"
- Sebastian

"Visually stimulating and cleverly academic... Young readers will enjoy the wit and humor of main character Aldo Zelnick."
— *ForeWord Reviews*

"Cahoots is a funny mystery that will surprise you. READ IT! You'll LOVE IT!"
- Mattias

"*Bogus* is the second graphic novel featuring the irrepressible Aldo Zelnick, kid detective and linguist extraordinaire. Aldo is a great hero for kids because he is exactly that: another believable kid. Pretty wonderful when you stop to examine him, after all. The comic illustrations keep the pages turning, as does the fast-moving story. Kids will love to collect all the letters of the alphabet as discovered by Aldo Zelnick."
— *Midwest Book Review*

"This is a fun series that my students adore."
— Katherine Sokolowski, 5th grade teacher

"My students and I are really enjoying *Artsy-Fartsy*. I think the children can identify with Aldo. I introduced *Artsy-Fartsy* to the other fourth grade grammar and composition teacher, and she has used the book as well. We like to use good literature in our teaching, and this year we used *Artsy-Fartsy* to emphasize 'voice' to our students. We also asked the students to identify thoughts and emotions used in the story. We are looking forward to the continuing adventures of Aldo, his friends and family."

- Carol Gorman, 4th grade teacher

"My class and I loved Artsy-Fartsy. It was the best book of 3rd grade."

- Tanner

"I am completely charmed by this series. The drawings and text have the quality of simultaneously being appealing to children and also amusing for adults. A big strength here is in the development of the characters. This is wonderful, since this is going to be an A to Z series and we'll have plenty of time to get to know them better. These are individuals with staying power. With the sketchbook comes a wonderful, not-overstated message of allowing Aldo to be himself and follow his creativity. Bravo!"

- Jean Hanson

"...a must for your elementary school reader."

— Christy, Reader's Cove bookstore

"My children (14, 9, 6, and 3) all enjoy the Aldo Zelnick series. Our 6-year-old boy is using them to read and understand new words. Our 9-year-old girl enjoys the humor and fun. Our 3-year-old enjoys hearing the silly stories and laughing with the rest of the family. And I've even seen our 14-year-old girl with a self-satisfied smile, putting the copy back on the shelf so as not to get caught doing something as uncool as reading a kids' book. And my wife and I enjoy the imaginative fun and wry wit in each tale.

"Can we extend the alphabet with some other letters so we can have more than 26 books in this series?"

- Chris Hutchinson

Dumbstruck

AN ALDO ZELNICK COMIC NOVEL

Written by Karla Oceanak

Illustrated by Kendra Spanjer

BAILIWICK PRESS

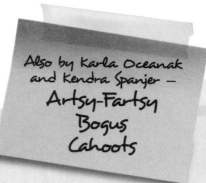

Also by Karla Oceanak
and Kendra Spanjer —
Artsy-Fartsy
Bogus
Cahoots

The Dum Dum wrapper on the back cover is used with permission from Spangler Candy Company, www.dumdumpops.com.

Published by:
Bailiwick Press
309 East Mulberry Street
Fort Collins, Colorado 80524
(970) 672-4878
Fax: (970) 672-4731
www.bailiwickpress.com
www.aldozelnick.com

Manufactured by:
Friesens Corporation, Altona, Canada
August 2011
Job # 67512

Book design by:
Launie Parry
Red Letter Creative
www.red-letter-creative.com

ISBN 978-1-934649-16-9

Library of Congress Control Number: 2011911699

20 19 18 17 16 15 14 13 12 11   7 6 5 4 3 2 1

Dearest Aldo –
A back-to-school sketchbook
for my darling grandson.
Keep discovering your creativity!
Your dyed-in-the-wool* fan,
Goosy

ALDO,

Hope you dig* the Ds
as much as I do.

Mr. Mot

WHO'S WHO

ME—ALDO ZELNICK. HOW D'YA LIKE MY 5TH GRADE SCHOOL PHOTO?

MY BEST FRIEND, JACK. HEY, WHAT'S HE DOING WITH GLUE AND A ROCK?

DANNY. HE TALKS WITH HIS HANDS.

MY OTHER FRIEND, ABIGAIL, A.K.A. BEE.

MS. MUNROE, MY NEW ART TEACHER (UNFORTUNATELY).

MR. MOT, THOU AREN'T AS BEAUTIFUL AS THOU ART WISE.

MY GRANDMA, GOOSY. PAINTS. SCULPTS. HURLS.

TOMMY GELLER. BULLY TURNED ART AFICIONADO.

MY SUPER-JOCK BROTHER, TIMOTHY.

SASHA, TIMOTHY'S NEW GIRLFRIEND. EW.

MY MOM & DAD.

MY DOG, MAX. DON'T BE SAD, MAXIE, I'LL ALWAYS LOVE YOU BEST.

BACON BOY, MY COMIC CHARACTER.

(My name's Aldo Zelnick, and besides being a basic 10-year-old, I write and draw sketchbooks. I've already finished 3 other ones. No big deal. Whenever you see this *, you can look in the Word Gallery at the back of the book to see what the word means.)

PENCIL PUSHERS

Making a kid shop for school supplies is like making a bad guy pick out his own handcuffs. It's cruel and unusual punishment!

According to my delusional* mother, lots of kids <u>enjoy</u> picking out glue sticks, folders, and index cards. Because life just doesn't get more fun than a 3-ring binder, is that it? Here's what I think: Shiny new notebooks are just grown-ups' way of trying to distract us kids from the fact that summer vacation is over and so are our lives.

My family just got home a couple of days ago from our trip to Minnesota, and this morning, after my brother Timothy's football practice, Dad dragged us to the store.

As it turns out, the only thing worse than shopping for school supplies is shopping for school supplies 3 days before school starts...because there's hardly anything left!

FOR EXAMPLE: HERE'S ALL THE GLUE THERE WAS.

ELMER'S WAS HERE.

So we were at the store, and Dad was standing at the end of the aisle with the shopping cart. He was holding my supply list and reading it to me one thing at a time. My job was to go find the item and put it in the shopping cart.

Timothy doesn't have a list. Unfair! Apparently, when you're in high school you get to decide for yourself which school supplies you need. Timothy tossed a pack of pens and a bag of sunflower seeds into the cart then took off for the sports department to pet the footballs or something.

So there I was, walking up and down that aisle of terribleness, trying to find folders without kitties or glitter on the cover, when I noticed a boy in a blue t-shirt who was also digging through the leftover debris* on the store shelves.

I caught his eye. "Did you find any boy folders?" I asked him.

With an embarrassed shrug, he showed me the folder he was holding. It had a horse picture on its cover. He pointed at the horse then stuck his finger inside his mouth, in a "this is so gross I might puke" gesture.

"Yup," I said. "Ponies. Hurl city."

I returned to Dad to tell him we needed to try a different store, but Dad wasn't noticing my annoyedness because he was too busy talking to a mom who was also holding a list.

"Aldo, this is Mrs. Peterson," said Dad. "That boy in the blue shirt is her son, Danny. He's in your grade. He'll be at Dana Elementary this year too."

Mrs. Peterson walked up behind Danny and tapped him twice on the shoulder. He turned to her, and the two of them started to communicate with their hands, fast and furious. This summer Timothy and I invented secret hand signals when we were trying to prank our Minnesota cousins, but Danny and his mom—wow, they had a much more elaborate system.

Finally Danny turned to me and gave me a "gangsta hands" signal. I looked at his mom and raised my eyebrows.

"Danny's deaf, Aldo," said Mrs. Peterson. "He's asking you 'What's up?' in American Sign Language."

"Oh, tell him I'm good," I said to her. I stupidly made a double thumbs-up—then shoved my hands into my pockets.

"Danny would like you to tell <u>him</u>," said Mrs. Peterson. "He's good at lip-reading, so if you look at him while you talk, it helps him understand." (While she was speaking, Mrs. Peterson kept talking with her hands, too, so Danny could be in on the conversation, I guess.)

BTW...if you can read this, you are WAY too close!

I turned to Danny. "Oh, I'm OK, I mean, we're at the store getting school supplies...so say goodbye to summer...uh, I mean, you don't actually have to <u>say</u> goodbye...well, it's just that my best friend, Jack, and I have a fort...," I blathered.

What was wrong with me???

Danny sign-languaged something to his mother. She smiled but also gave him the mom-look that means, "If you can't say anything nice, don't say anything at all."

"He says he...thinks your hair is unique," said Mrs. Peterson. "Will we see you at the back-to-school ice cream social?"

"Wouldn't miss it!" said Dad. We waved goodbye to Danny and his mom and went to get Timothy so we could check out then go to another store.

HERE'S WHERE WE FOUND HIM. UGH.

ALWAYS TAKE TIME TO STOP AND SMELL THE FOOTBALLS.

In the car, I clamped my hands tight over my ears to see what it would be like not to hear Timothy belching in the back seat or cars whooshing past us or Dad singing along to "Me and Julio Down by the Schoolyard." (Yup. This is my life.) It sounded like the inside of one of those giant seashells.

NICE! TIME FOR AN UPGRADE.

Later on, at home, Dad handed me my school supplies to put in my backpack. "Ponies, huh?" he said. "Good choice for getting the girls to think you're the sensitive type." And he winked and handed me...the pony folder that Danny and I had gagged over!

"Hey...I didn't pick this!" I protested.

"Don't be embarrassed, sport," said Dad. "I know you got to be buddies with the horses at your cousins' farm. Guys can like ponies too."

I glared and stomped up to my room, where I shoved the pony folder under my bed. Danny must have snuck it into our shopping cart at the store. Now I just need to devise* a way to embarrass him back.

DON'T FEEL BAD, CUTE LITTLE PONY. IT'S NOT YOU, IT'S ALDO.

I'M BEING PETTED BY A PIECE OF BACON.

AT LEAST I GOT NEW ART SUPPLIES WHEN WE WERE SHOPPING. IT MADE THE DAY SEEM A LITTLE LESS DASTARDLY.*

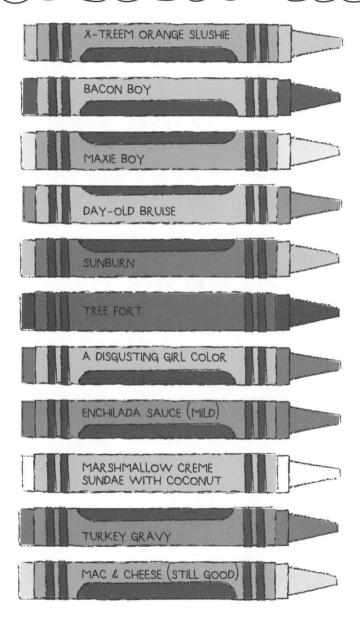

X-TREEM ORANGE SLUSHIE

BACON BOY

MAXIE BOY

DAY-OLD BRUISE

SUNBURN

TREE FORT

A DISGUSTING GIRL COLOR

ENCHILADA SAUCE (MILD)

MARSHMALLOW CREME SUNDAE WITH COCONUT

TURKEY GRAVY

MAC & CHEESE (STILL GOOD)

BUT I SHOULD BE IN CHARGE OF NAMING THE CRAYONS.

HOW DO I DETEST* THEE? LET ME COUNT THE WAYS

(Or, 7 Things About Going Back to School That Fill Me with Dread* and Despair*)

1. School takes up 7 and a half hours a day. This is a disgrace.*

2. I have to get up at 7 o'clock. In the morning!

3. My mom makes me wear "decent*" clothes instead of what I like to wear.

WHAT I LIKE TO WEAR = WHATEVER'S ON TOP

4. The cafeteria serves dinky,* kindergartener-
    sized portions.

5. I have to walk to AND from school. This is
    EXERCISE. OUTSIDE. In the FRESH AIR.

6. Max feels sad when he's home alone all day!

7. Homework.
    Need I say more?

WE ALL SCREAM

Every August, a few days before school
starts up again, Dana Elementary puts on an ice
cream social. The idea is that families come to the
school after dinner so us kids can bring our school
supplies to our classrooms, find our desks, and
meet our teachers. The ice cream is just a bribe.

The good news is that Jack and I are in the same class this year. The bad news is...school itself. I mean, I'm a good student and all, but c'mon. Which would you rather have—school, or endless summer vacation? <u>I thought so!</u>

Anyway, Jack and I took our school supplies to our classroom. Our teacher, Mr. Krug, was there to introduce himself so we wouldn't have stranger danger on the first day of school. We also found our lockers and dumped our stuff inside them.

"I think we're going to like Mr. Krug," said Jack on the way to the gym, where the ice cream was. "Did you notice that he smiles with his eyes?"

"Uh...no. That's dumb. But I did notice that he keeps a big jar of Jolly Ranchers behind his desk. He must be a rewarder! I love <u>rewarder</u> teachers."

HM. MR. KRUG'S HAIR IS MISSING RIGHT WHERE THE SHOWER SPRAY HITS A PERSON'S HEAD.
NOTE TO SELF: CONTINUE SHOWERING AS LITTLE AS POSSIBLE.

HEY – I JUST REALIZED HIS WHOLE NAME IS DOUG KRUG.

"Remember Mrs. Muñoz, in first grade?" asked Jack. "She gave us a goldfish cracker every time we did anything good, like say please or push in our chair."

"Yes!" I said. "I spent the entire year in the hallway, throwing kids' coats onto the floor just so I could hang them up again."

We found our parents in the rows of chairs in the gym and sat by them. The deal with the ice cream social is that you have to listen to Principal Dobrowski talk before the ice cream part.

"Welcome to a new school year!" he boomed into the microphone. All the parents clapped. My mom stood and whistled. "Blah, blah, blah...," he continued.

Another guy was standing on stage, a little ways away from Mr. Dobrowski. He was sign-languaging everything the principal said. So I looked for Danny and spotted him with his mom a few rows ahead of us. Danny turned around and signaled something to me—a funny two-fingered wave by his head followed by a down motion with the same hand. In return I gave him the universal "What the heck are you talking about?" signal. →

"And before we dig into the ice cream," Mr. Dobrowski finally said, "allow me to introduce Ms. Munroe, our new art teacher."

A lady with dark hair and skin the color of turkey gravy stepped forward. She was taller than Mr. Dobrowski, so she adjusted the microphone to make it higher and bonked herself on the chin. The crowd giggled.

"The secret of life...," she paused, "is in art." Her voice was crunchy but also smooth. It sounded like butter brickle ice cream. "I hope to inspire you to become as passionate about art as I am. So we're going to start off the year with a contest. The grand prize is a mystery gift and lunch from the take-out restaurant of your choice, my treat." Now the kids were clapping and whistling.

"What's wrong with you?" Jack whispered.

All of a sudden, I had begun to feel sick. The weird sensations that were creeping inside me must have been showing on the outside too.

My stomach felt throw-uppish and my throat seemed frozen. I couldn't even answer Jack. I had to step outside for a gulp of air.

And you wanna know what's so completely unbelievable that my brain might explode now that I'm realizing it?

I didn't have any ice cream at the ice cream social.

YOU KNOW HOW SOME PEOPLE GET BRAIN FREEZE WHEN THEY EAT ICE CREAM? I GET BRAIN EXPLOSION WHEN I DON'T EAT ICE CREAM.

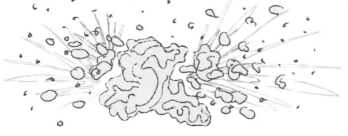

Weird! I've heard of the 24-hour flu, but is there such a thing as the 10-minute flu? Or maybe I was feeling strange about the art contest? I don't know what that was all about. Welp, I'm at home now, writing this. I'm OK, but I think I'll go to bed early. Tomorrow's the last day of summer vacation, and I want to be able to lounge the day away with a good appetite.

STAYIN' ALIVE

No. WE DON'T REALLY USE THEM FOR STOOLS. THAT WOULD BE ABSURD.

EASY, BIG FELLA. I DIDN'T INVENT THE WORD.

This morning Jack and I rode our bikes to the convenience store for last-day-of-summer-vacation Slushies and snacks. Then we took the feast to our fort under the giant pine tree. Bee was already there, nibbling a delicious (NOT!) daikon radish* from her garden. We all just sat there, munching and chillaxing.

"Aldo, did you notice that new kid at the ice cream social last night—the one talking in sign language to his parents?" asked Jack after a while.

"Yeah. I met him the other day. His name's Danny."

"What did you think of his haircut?" said Jack. "I kinda liked it."

"Hey, I've met Danny!" said Bee. "His family just moved here this summer. They joined my toadstool group."

"You're actually in a group for people who like mushrooms...," I said in disbelief.*

"My <u>homeschool</u> group, you doofus.* It's a bunch of homeschool families who get together for game nights and field trips. Things like that."

"Maybe if I let my hair grow a little longer...," continued Jack.

HM. THAT MIGHT NOT BE THE BEST IDEA...

"Wait a sec," I said, pointing at Bee, "you're saying that you don't have to go to school tomorrow!"

"Duh. Bee's homeschooled," said Jack. "She told us that before."

BEST-CASE SCENARIO: JACK LOOKS LIKE A DROWNED RAT.

WORST-CASE SCENARIO: THE ZOO CALLS. THEY'RE MISSING A MONKEY.

Oh yeah. I did kinda remember, now that he said it. "But she told us during the summer," I reminded Jack. "And my summer ears don't really listen to anything that has to do with school. And you—," I turned to Bee, "you get to stay <u>home</u> every day?" I was getting so apoplectic I almost choked on my chicken taquito.

I THINK I'LL STUDY CARTOON NETWORK TODAY, MOTHER DEAR.

YES, AND AFTER THAT, PERHAPS A LITTLE REST.

(THIS IS VIVI, BEE'S LITTLE SISTER)

"So, what are you gonna make for the school art contest, Aldo?" interrupted Jack, trying to keep the conversation light and summery.

"There's a contest?" asked Bee.

"We have a new art teacher," explained Jack. "She wants to get everyone excited about art, so she's starting off the year with a contest. First prize is a mystery gift. And lunch, but probably not peanut butter sandwiches..."

"A contest! That's so cool," said Bee. "I wish I could do it."

Oh yeah. The new art teacher.

"I might not even enter that dumb contest," I said, remembering how I've been teased at school about my drawings. Part of my brain also thought: *Good thing Bee can't enter the contest. She's a <u>great</u> drawer.*

"So Aldo...did you see the new accessory we added to the fort while you were on vacation?" said Jack-the-subject-changer.

"Yeah, we've been dying for you to notice!" said Bee, who quickly climbed the bottom tree limb.

I looked up to see what she was doing and spotted something white hanging from a twig. She fiddled with it and out came...disco* music! Ack.

Bee and Jack stood to wiggle and sing along:

"Well you can tell by the way I use my walk, I'm a woman's man—no time to talk..."

"Alrighty then! A CD player...and dancing!" I said.

"Time to go swimming." And I scurried out from under the fort tree and sped over to the neighborhood swimming pool to dunk* myself in the cold water. (I mean, Bee's our friend and all, but that doesn't mean we should be dancing with her. Does it? Sheesh.)

The Truth About Homeschool

by Abigail Goode

I saw the picture you drew on page 30. For your information, ALDO, I don't watch TV during homeschool.

My mom does sometimes bring snacks to me and my little sister, Vivi, while we're doing our school work. Which is just one reason why homeschool is bodacious.

But homeschool is still school. I learn just as much as you do at regular school.

And one more thing, in case you're wondering:
Sometimes homeschool kids do their basic subjects at home, like English and math, but go to a regular school for special classes, like foreign languages or art.

This must be what Danny's doing.
Sounds kinda fun, actually...

School is for fish!

Here's a test. Can you do this math problem?

240)5280

I can.

DEAD MEN WALKIN'

Welp, I made it through the first day of school. Sort of.

For breakfast, to soften the blow, Dad made us chocolate-chip pancakes and bacon. Mom, she made us pose for a picture.

TIMOTHY—FIRST DAY OF HIGH SCHOOL; ME—FIRST DAY OF 5TH GRADE. (MY MOM TRIED TO WIPE OFF MY FACE BUT I TOLD HER IT WAS FINE. UH...YEAH.)

Then, with my head low and my spirits even lower, I started the 10-minute walk to school. After a block or so I stopped at Jack's house, like I always do, and he and I walked the rest of the way together.

"Chocolate-chip pancakes for breakfast?" asked Jack, kicking a stone down the street in front of us.

"Yup," I said, shuffling up to the rock and taking my turn to kick it ahead.

"How'd you know?"

"Lucky guess."

I could see the school in the distance now. Kids and parents and teachers clumped excitedly around the building, like they were aliens and Dana Elementary was the mothership. Ugh.

I sighed. "At least we're in 5th this year."
5th graders are the oldest kids at our school.

"Yeah. And we're finally in the same class!"
said Jack. The last couple of years we'd had
different teachers. Whoever decides class lists should
know that separating best friends is uber-dumb.

Maybe the chocolate chips were starting to
deceive* my brain, but I was just beginning
to feel a tiny bit better about school
when I kicked the rock good and hard and
it skittered under a bush.

"I'll get it," I said, and I knelt down and
grabbed the rock. As I stood, I felt a ninja-sharp
sting on my right face.

"Owwwch!" I yelled. "Something bit me."

"Was it a bee?" Jack came close to inspect.
He knows I'm allergic to bees. "It musta been
hungry for chocolate. Your cheek's turning red.
C'mon. I'll go with you to the nurse's office."

Sure enough, I'd been stung. Nurse Dolores called my mom and told her she was giving me some medicine. "Other than a little swelling, he's fine," she said into the phone. "He's had a pretty mild reaction, so he can stay. I'm sure he doesn't want to miss the first day of school!"

Groan. So here's how I looked during my first class of my first day of 5th grade:

THE STUNG SIDE OF MY FACE LOOKED LIKE MR. POTATO HEAD...

I'M NOT A ROOT VEGETABLE, I'M A HUMAN BEING!

...BOX TO HIDE MY EMBARRASSMENT NOT INCLUDED.

SHE GAVE ME
AN ART ATTACK

And guess what my first class of 5th grade was? You guessed it. Art. While the new teacher, Ms. Munroe, introduced herself, I slouched down in my chair and hid my puffy face behind my sketchbook.

She told us we're going to start the year by studying pop art. (For a second I thought she said pop-tart. Normally this would make me hungry, but instead I felt kinda sick and weird—definitely <u>not</u> hungry. *Stupid bees*, I thought.)

Danny was sitting next to me in art class, along with the interpreter guy who was at the ice cream social. He watched and listened to Ms. Munroe then sign-languaged everything she said.

STRAWBERRY WITH FROSTING. MY FAVORITE.

SOMETIMES MY MOM BUYS THE ORGANIC WHOLE-WHEAT KIND WITH NO FROSTING. IT'S ABOMINABLE!

THE GOOD NEWS FOR US IS THAT INTERPRETING ALSO WORKS IN REVERSE:

ART.

"I'll bet many of you have seen the famous Campbell's Soup can paintings by Andy Warhol." Ms. Munroe walked around holding up a picture in a book for all of us to see. "This is pop art. It's

about taking popular things that are part of our everyday lives and presenting them in an artful way," she said as her giraffey legs carried her around the room, "—a way that makes us consider them more deeply."

As she said the word "deeply," she lunged downward for effect...and lost her balance. She tipped sideways, and just when it looked like she would topple over, lurched herself upright.

That's when I found myself standing next to Ms. Munroe at the front of the room! I don't remember leaving my seat and rushing to her side, but that's what must have happened.

"Even if art isn't your favorite subject, my clumsiness will entertain you this year," she said, and she bowed. While everyone else laughed and clapped, she whispered to me, "Thank you for helping, Aldo," and she nodded at the book she'd dropped on the floor. I picked it up, and when I handed it to her, our fingertips touched. I felt a shock of static electricity, and my arms got all goose-bumpy.

As my legs returned my red, swollen face to its chair, Danny winked at me. He made an L with his fingers and put his hand to his forehead. *Pony folder*, I remembered. It was still under my bed.

Then, thankfully, Ms. Munroe had us take an everyday object from our backpacks and draw it. Drawing always calms me down. Jack tried to draw a piece of dolomite* he had in his pocket, but his drawing turned out more turd-like than rock-like.

I was annoyed to notice that Danny made a cool sketch of a dime. Here's mine:

DEVIL SQUARES.
THE DELECTABLE* SNACKS GIRLS TRY TO HIDE FROM BOYS BY PUTTING THEM IN BOXES LABELED "LITTLE DEBBIE."

Before the bell rang, Ms. Munroe told us more about the art contest. "Create something in the pop-art style," she said. "It can be a drawing, a painting, or a sculpture. We'll be practicing pop-art together in class, but your contest entry is something you'll create on your own, at home.

At the end of this month, everyone's work will
be displayed in an art show at the mall. You
and your families will be invited to an evening
premiere...and that's
when judges will choose
the winner of the
special lunch and this
mystery prize."

   And she
reached inside her
desk drawer
and pulled out:

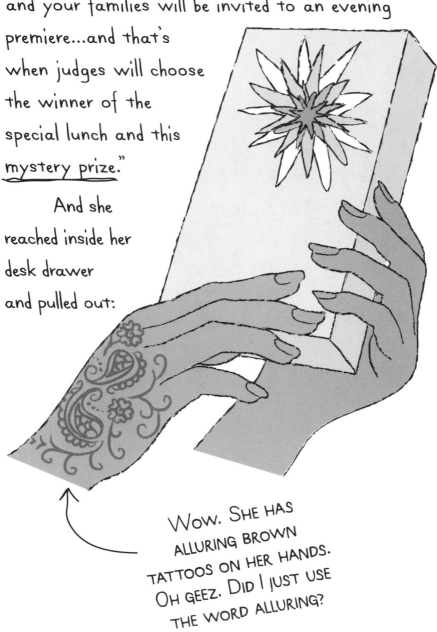

Wow. She has
alluring brown
tattoos on her hands.
Oh geez. Did I just use
the word alluring?

Ms. Munroe passed the box around the room. We got to feel how heavy it was and hear how it sounded when we shook it. It was silent. Whatever's in that box, it's packed up good and tight, because it doesn't make any noise at all.

I dunno. I've always been embarrassed that I'm the tiniest bit artsy-fartsy. Tommy Geller used to tease me at school about my drawings, but now he's in 6th grade, at middle school, so I guess I don't have to worry about him...

And maybe it's just the bee poison talking, but there's something about art class this year that makes me want to unleash my full artistic power.

Yup. I'm gonna do it.

I'm gonna win this contest.

CONTEST IDEA #1:
THE DAGWOOD*

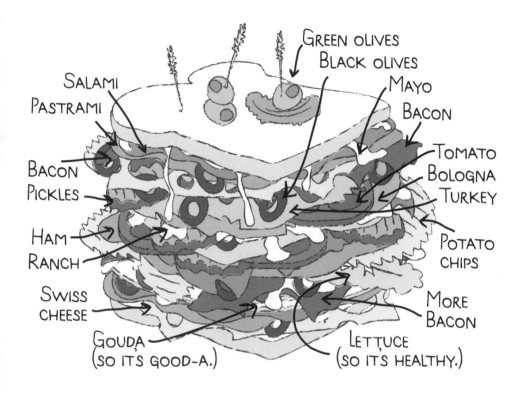

SALAMI
PASTRAMI

BACON
PICKLES

HAM
RANCH

SWISS
CHEESE

GOUDA
(SO IT'S GOOD-A.)

GREEN OLIVES
BLACK OLIVES

MAYO
BACON

TOMATO
BOLOGNA
TURKEY

POTATO
CHIPS

MORE
BACON

LETTUCE
(SO IT'S HEALTHY.)

My dad calls this a Dagwood sandwich. I
don't know why. We like to make Dagwoods on
Sunday afternoons during football season. For
some reason, football fans get to eat copious
snacks. Anyway, I could draw a giant Dagwood
for the contest and color it in. More interesting
than a can of tomato soup, right?

UNFORTUNATELY, IT'S NO LONGER MIDSUMMER

Today my word-nerd friend and neighbor Mr. Mot came to my class wearing tights. And not the superhero kind, either.

"Lord, what fools these mortals be...," whispered a gravelly old voice at my side, and I looked over to see him crouching next to my desk in a crazy cape, hat, and tights. "Hello, Aldo."

Sometimes Mr. Mot volunteers at Dana Elementary. He helps with Englishy things, like the spelling bee and the book fair and stuff like that. Apparently Mr. Krug invited him to our class today.

"Class, we are lucky to have with us Milton Melville Mot," announced Mr. Krug. "Mr. Mot is a former English teacher, and he is here to help us with our unit on *A Midsummer Night's Dream*, which is a famous play by William Shakespeare."

Mr. Mot leaped on top of Mr. Krug's desk
and began waving his arms and spouting nonsense:

"Thou speak'st aright;
I am that merry
wanderer of the night.
I jest to oberon and
make him smile
when I a fat and
bean-fed horse beguile..."

I MADE MR. MOT WRITE
THIS PART DOWN SO YOU
WOULDN'T THINK I WAS
MAKING IT UP. I KNOW...
IT SOUNDS LIKE I MADE IT
UP. BUT IT DOES MAKE ME
HUNGRY FOR A BURRITO.

Mr. Mot told us that *A Midsummer Night's Dream* is a funny story about mistaken identities and characters falling in love with each other. *Oh great.* But he promised us that by the end of the month we'd be laughing our heads off and that Shakespeare would be one of our favorite comedians. Let's just say I'm dubious.*

Oh, and he assigned all of us parts to read as we learn the play. He gave me some guy called Nick Bottom. He's a weaver.

At least I don't have to be a fairy like Jack does.

HEY, I'M OBERON. <u>KING</u> OF THE FAIRIES, DUDE.

ALL THE STUFF I HAVE TO DO

Grown-ups seem to think that kids have it easy. I beg to differ.* I'm copying down my schedule here to prove to you how little time kids have for relaxation.

8:15 ARRIVE AT PAIN-A ELEMENTARY AND ARRANGE MY STUFF IN MY LOCKER.

YUP, LOCKERS. 5TH GRADERS ARE **THAT** COOL.

8:25 BELL RINGS. PRINCIPAL DOBROWSKI BLABS ON THE LOUDSPEAKER.

WAH WAH-WAH MWAH-WAH-WAH-HA-WAH

THEN WE STAND AND PLEDGE.

8:30 SPANISH (HARD).

¿QUÉ?

OR

ART (I TOTALLY RULE).

9:20 GRAMMAR. FALL BACK ASLEEP. (SILENT Zs.)

10:10 LANGUAGE ARTS. READING AND WRITING. SEMI-INTERESTING.

11:00 BAND. ♪

OR

P.E.?! AT THIS HOUR?! I'M PRACTICALLY STARVING AS IT IS.

11:50 LUNCH! MY FAVORITE SUBJECT.

(ALTHOUGH, AS I'VE MENTIONED, THE HOT LUNCH PORTIONS ARE DIMINUTIVE.*)

12:20 RECESS. FRESH AIR.

BUT I **AM** THE KING OF 4-SQUARE.

12:45 MATH.

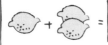

EASY-PEEZY LEMON SQUEEZY.

1:35 SCIENCE.

MMM. PLANTS.

WHATEVERUS MAXIMUS.

2:25 HISTORY.

DEAD PEOPLE.

3:15... BELL! FINALLY.

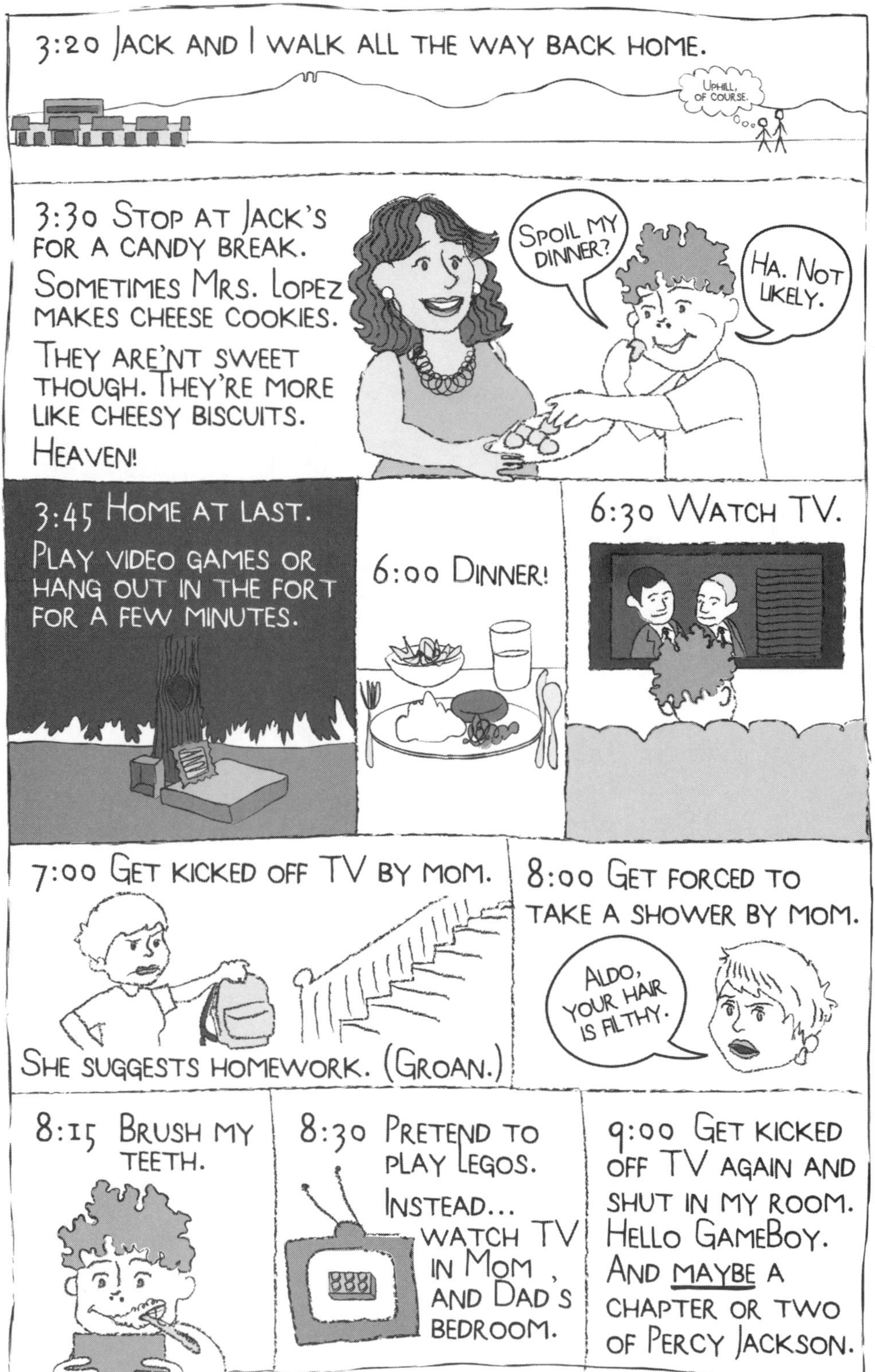
3:20 JACK AND I WALK ALL THE WAY BACK HOME.
UPHILL, OF COURSE.
3:30 STOP AT JACK'S FOR A CANDY BREAK.
SOMETIMES MRS. LOPEZ MAKES CHEESE COOKIES.
THEY AREN'T SWEET THOUGH. THEY'RE MORE LIKE CHEESY BISCUITS.
HEAVEN!
SPOIL MY DINNER?
HA. NOT LIKELY.
3:45 HOME AT LAST.
PLAY VIDEO GAMES OR HANG OUT IN THE FORT FOR A FEW MINUTES.
6:00 DINNER!
6:30 WATCH TV.
7:00 GET KICKED OFF TV BY MOM.
SHE SUGGESTS HOMEWORK. (GROAN.)
8:00 GET FORCED TO TAKE A SHOWER BY MOM.
ALDO, YOUR HAIR IS FILTHY.
8:15 BRUSH MY TEETH.
8:30 PRETEND TO PLAY LEGOS.
INSTEAD... WATCH TV IN MOM AND DAD'S BEDROOM.
9:00 GET KICKED OFF TV AGAIN AND SHUT IN MY ROOM.
HELLO GAMEBOY.
AND MAYBE A CHAPTER OR TWO OF PERCY JACKSON.

BEE A CONTENDER

On the way home from school today, Jack and I swung by the convenience store for Slushies then brought them to our fort. It was a warm afternoon, so if you didn't know better, you might think it was still summer vacation. Except that our backpacks were stuffed with homework and I kept yawning from getting up at the crack of dawn!

I MISS SUMMER.

"I worked on a drawing of a sandwich for the art contest," I yawn-said.

"That's cool," said Jack. "I'm thinking about doing something with Dungeons & Dragons.*"

Jack started playing Dungeons & Dragons while I was on vacation last month. Tommy Geller invited Jack to play in his D&D league after they realized they were both rock hounds and it turned out that Tommy, who helped us find a lost, non-bogus diamond ring this summer, wasn't <u>totally</u> a bad kid.

"But that's not really pop-art because Dungeons & Dragons isn't really <u>popular</u>," I said.

"Yes it is. Millions of people play it worldwide."

"Yeah, well, millions of people are <u>dumb</u> worldwide." Usually when Jack and I tell each other that something is dumb, we only <u>kinda</u> mean it. But today I <u>mostly</u> meant it. Jack hadn't asked me to play D&D even once!

"Maybe you should come to D&D this week with me and Tommy," said Jack-the-mind-reader.

"Hmph. Maybe."

Just then Bee flitted into the fort with her big news.

"Guess what!" she buzzed. "I signed up at Dana Elementary for some classes! I get to take art and P.E. there, just like Danny, and music and Spanish, too!"

"Oh boy, you get to go to school!" I said with pretend excitement.

"Hey, that means you can be in the art contest!" said Jack with authentic excitement. "Aldo drew a sandwich!"

My sandwich idea didn't sound so cool when Jack said it. Suddenly I didn't feel like telling everyone what I was making for the contest. Suddenly it felt like a good idea to keep it a secret. And suddenly it felt like a <u>bad</u> idea to have a friend who's a girl who goes to my school—a girl who's a good artist, especially.

"Oh I'm not entering that stupid sandwich," I said. "That was just my warm-up idea. Time to go work on my <u>real</u> idea."

I crawled out from under the fort tree only to see Timothy and Jack's next-door neighbor girl, Sasha, swinging together on the playground at the park. That's right—Timothy, a 9th grader, was swinging on the swings...with a girl. They were giggling and trying to see who could go the highest, and just as I was turning around in disgust,* Timothy did a backflip off the swing and landed like you'd expect a Super-Jock to land (in other words, perfectly). He was showing off for Sasha!

Sorry you had to see that, Max.

CONTEST IDEA #2: SLUSHIE POWER

I filled an *actual* Slushie cup with layers of modeling clay. Because Slushies are popular and clay is easy to smoosh into shape.

Hmm... It's not bad, but I think this might be one of those things that looks better in your mind than in does in real life. Like Turkish Delight,* that delicacy* from Narnia.

POP-SLUSHIE
(PRETTY CONVINCING, ISN'T IT.)

RED CLAY ↘

YELLOW CLAY →

BROWN CLAY →

GREEN CLAY →

BLACK CLAY ↗

MORE GREEN →

...BECAUSE IF YOU DON'T LAYER YOUR SLUSHIE, YOU'RE NOT REALLY A SLUSHIE AFICIONADO

WHAT TURKISH DELIGHT SEEMED LIKE IN THE BOOK WAS A LOT DIFFERENT THAN WHAT IT WAS REALLY LIKE WHEN MY DAD AND I MADE IT. (CLOSER TO BOOGERS.)

NOT TO TOOT MY OWN HORN...

WA-WAH!
WAAAHMP!

At my school, 5th graders get to choose: sing in the choir or play in the band. I picked band because, welp, at least you get to sit down when you have a concert.

Today I had band for the first time. We got to try out the different instruments to see which one we liked best. The band teacher, Mrs. Dulcet, talked a little about each one, and she demonstrated how they're played. Then she set them out for us to try.

At the end of class, Jack said he was gonna take trombone. Bee loved the drums. Me, I chose the trumpet because it has cool levers and holes for letting the spit out.

BEE WAS IN BAND CLASS, BUT DANNY WASN'T. I WONDER WHAT DEAF PEOPLE THINK ABOUT MUSIC? YOU CAN'T TASTE IT OR SMELL IT OR SEE IT. YOU CAN <u>KINDA</u> FEEL IT, BUT THE ONLY WAY TO REALLY HEAR IT IS TO HEAR IT, RIGHT?

At dinner tonight, when I told my parents and Timothy which instrument I'd picked, Dad walked over to the coat closet and pulled out a little black case. He opened it, and inside sat...a flute.

"Here's your instrument, sport," he said. "Timothy chose it when he was in 5th grade."

"You picked the flute?" I said in astonishment.

"Yeah," Timothy chuckled. "The cutest girl in our class that year was Destiny, and she chose the flute. I wanted to sit next to her."

"Gross! Well, I'm not playing the flute. I shouldn't have to pay for your dumbness. Only girls play the stupid flute." I crossed my arms over my chest and scowled.

"Band instruments don't grow on trees, Aldo," said Mom. "We bought this one already, and it won't kill you to try it."

I started to throw a fit, but Dad raised his right finger and his left eyebrow—Zelnick Sign Language for "hang on a second."

"If you're still playing in the band next year and you want to try a different instrument," he said, "you can pick whatever you want. Until then, you're the proud owner of a barely used flute. I guess you could say it's your destiny.*"

I was the only Zelnick who didn't get a chuckle out of that one.

MY HEAD IS SPINNING

So there I sat in art class today, and Bee was there, too, looking all chipper and happy to be at school. When she waved at me, I pretended I had pencil dust in my eye and couldn't see her.

Ms. Munroe was explaining about some guy called Jasper Johns and his pop-art paintings of super simple stuff, like numbers and the American flag. While she talked, I concentrated on doodling* on the cover of my art notebook because whenever I looked up at her, I felt dizzy. It must be because she's so tall.

Ms. Munroe said that Jasper had a dream about painting the flag, so when he woke up, he actually did it. Only 48 stars though. What's up with that? And anybody can draw a <u>FLAG</u>, for Pete's sake.

I'd finally remembered to bring the pony folder to school! I'd used a black marker to write DANNY in big block letters on the cover, and I'd added a purple unicorn horn to the pony's head. (Because a unicorn is the only mammal more embarrassing than a pony.) Then, in the middle of art class, I walked over to Danny's desk and casually handed it to him. "You must've dropped this," I said.

Danny didn't blush, though—he smiled! "I was wondering when you'd get this back to me," he replied through his interpreter. "And here's something I found of yours." And he pulled a box of jumbo crayons labeled ALDO from his backpack and handed them to me!

"Hey!" I started to complain, but then I noticed all the other kids were staring at me and my brand-new 8-box of jumbo crayons. I didn't wanna get in trouble for yelling at the deaf kid, so I sat down. I spent the rest of art class trying to think of a way to get back at Danny.

"I hope you're having fun with your own pop-art projects," said Ms. Munroe just before the bell. "Oh, and I need volunteers to help make signs advertising the art show and contest to hang around the school. Who's willing to spend their recess making posters?"

My mouth made a big, stupid smile and my hand shot up in the air like it was suddenly filled with helium. *What are you doing?* I thought at my hand. Even Jack looked askance at me. "Recess!" he hissed. "4-square!"

Danny and Bee raised their hands too.

"Wonderful," said Ms. Munroe, lurching over near my desk. "So I'll see the 3 of you here in the art room right after lunch tomorrow?"

Danny said yes with his hand and Bee said yes with her voice, but when I tried to talk, nothing came out except a breathy, strangling noise. My voice had stopped working again!

So I went to see Nurse Dolores. She stuck a tongue depressor* in my mouth to check my throat. She also took my temperature. "Everything's normal!" she said.

"But I couldn't talk," I said, even though now I was talking just fine.

"If it happens again, get a drink of water."

Hmph. Why do grown-ups always seem to think that a drink of water can fix anything?

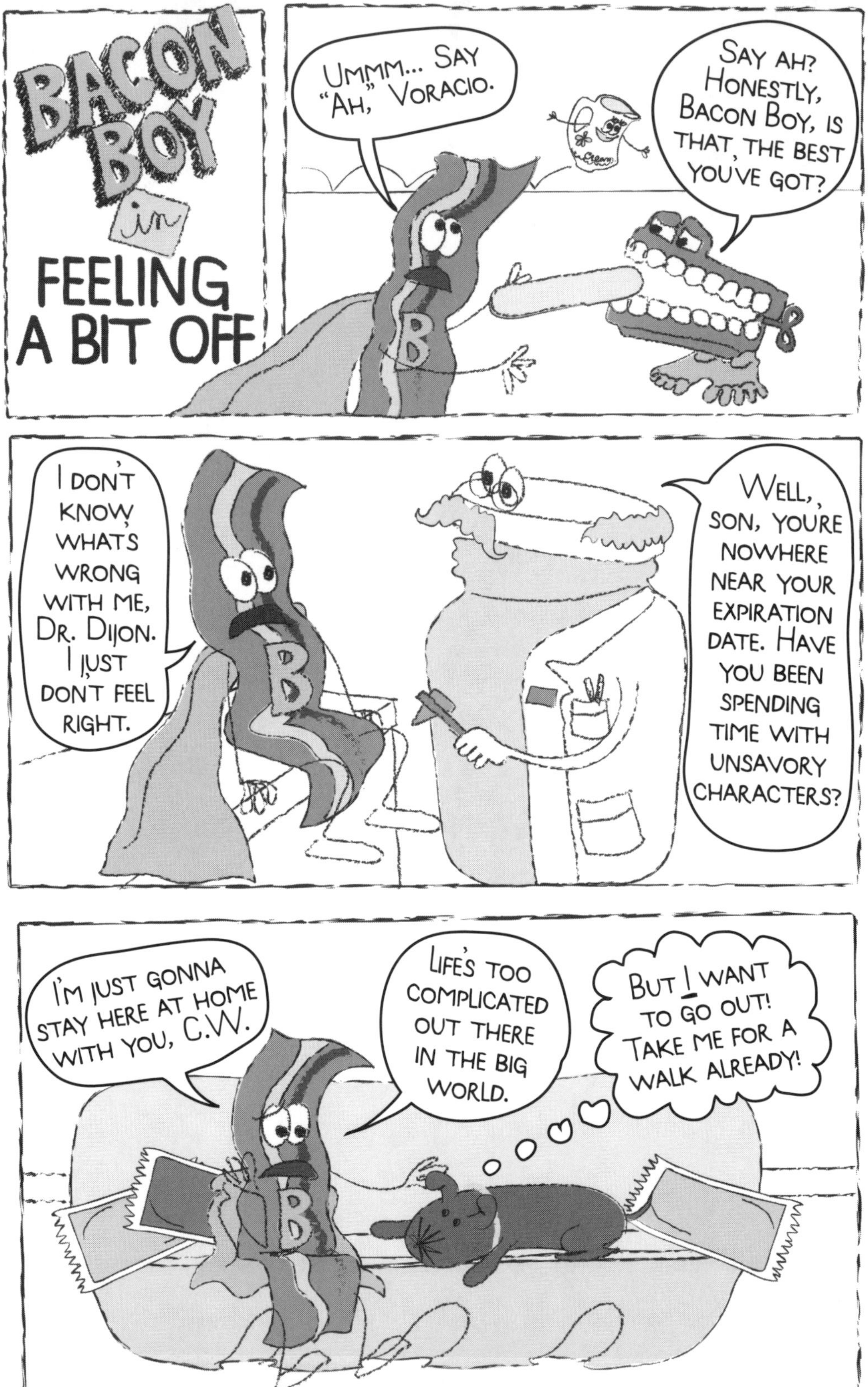
BACON BOY in
FEELING A BIT OFF
UMMM... SAY "AH," VORACIO.
SAY AH? HONESTLY, BACON BOY, IS THAT, THE BEST YOU'VE GOT?
I DON'T KNOW WHAT'S WRONG WITH ME, DR. DIJON. I JUST DON'T FEEL RIGHT.
WELL, SON, YOU'RE NOWHERE NEAR YOUR EXPIRATION DATE. HAVE YOU BEEN SPENDING TIME WITH UNSAVORY CHARACTERS?
I'M JUST GONNA STAY HERE AT HOME WITH YOU, C.W.
LIFE'S TOO COMPLICATED OUT THERE IN THE BIG WORLD.
BUT I WANT TO GO OUT! TAKE ME FOR A WALK ALREADY!

FOOL ME ONCE

That Shakespeare was one crazy dude.

Remember the play we're learning in language arts called *A Midsummer Night's Dream*? Turns out it's about a girl named Hermia (A) and a guy called Lysander (B). They like each other. The problem is that Hermia's dad (C) thinks Hermia should marry a different guy, Demetrius (D).

So Hermia and Lysander run away together. Meanwhile, Hermia's best friend, Helena (E), likes Demetrius, but he likes Hermia, even though she doesn't like him.

<u>Whatever.</u>

Then this bunch of fairies who live in the forest get involved. They use a love potion to try to make Demetrius fall in love with Helena, but they give it to Lysander by mistake, so then things get <u>really messed</u> up.

Mr. Mot was at school again today,
jumping around in his tights and helping everyone
read their lines.

Like I said before...this Nick character is a
weaver, but in the play I don't think he weaves
a darn thing. I get the distinct* feeling he's a
dunderhead.*

CONTEST IDEA #3:

DUH

A bacon painting! After all, what could be more popular than a pound of bacon?

SIGN, SIGN, EVERYWHERE A SIGN

Despite Jack's disapproval,* I went to the art room during recess today to make posters. When I got there, Bee, Danny, and Danny's interpreter were already there, but Ms. Munroe wasn't yet. And the mystery prize was sitting out on her desk, in all its shiny glory!

Danny ambled over and picked it up. He shook it. He cocked his ear to it, like he was listening to what it sounded like. Bee laughed. Danny waggled his eyebrows at her and her cheeks got pink. *Oh please.*

Danny set down the wrapped box so he could talk with his hands. "I bet it's an iPod," his interpreter translated for him. "What am <u>I</u> gonna do with an iPod?" His hands practically hypnotize you when he signs, the way they flick and pop. It's like watching those amazing hip-hop dancers on YouTube. His face and arms get really animated when he talks too.

68

I picked up the box to feel it again. "It's too heavy for an iPod," I said. "Maybe it's a book. Ugh. I bet it's some boring art book!"

At that point Ms. Munroe stumbled in, apologizing for being late. She told us each to tear a big piece of white paper off the giant school-sized rolls. She gave us cups of paint and brushes, and she wrote on the chalkboard what the posters should say. Then she got her own piece of paper and sat down next to us to make a poster too.

"So what are you making for the art contest, Danny?" she asked as she began painting in huge orange letters across the top of her poster.

Danny signed and his interpreter said, "A painting."

"Of what?" asked Bee.

"It's a buck," said Danny.

"How interesting!" said Ms. Munroe, glancing up to look at Danny while she spoke. By now she had orange paint streaked across her cheek. "The deer in the tractor company logo is very pop-art. What about you, Aldo?"

When she said my name, the "L" sounded like a cat's purr. I panicked!

DEER IN HEADLIGHTS*

"Uhhh...," I rasped. "I've got a few ideas..." Once again I could feel my throat tightening up, so I excused myself to get a drink from the water fountain. Bee rolled her eyes at me.

I stood in the hallway for a minute to collect myself. *What the heck was wrong with me?* When I got back to the art room, Bee was talking.

"Well, I like to draw," she said, "so I'm working on a drawing. It's a vacuum cleaner!"

"A vacuum cleaner?!" I said. I couldn't help myself. "That's really dumb."

*DISTOL?**

Everyone put down their brushes and stared at me (with their mouths agape) except Danny. He must have been too busy painting his poster to see his interpreter sign what I'd said. Note to self: Things you say in the privacy of your own fort might not be taken the right way when you say them in public.

RETRACT-O-VAC 5000

THAT'S DUMB

NOW HERE'S A VACUUM I COULD ACTUALLY USE.

71

"I can't wait to see your vacuum, Bee,"
said Ms. Munroe. "And Aldo, disparaging*
comments don't have a place in my classroom."

I felt about 2 inches tall. And my voice
stopped working again, so I couldn't even say
sorry. At the end of the poster-making time, guess
who Ms. Munroe chose to clean out the paint cups
and brushes.

STUDENT
ART SHOW
(AND)
CONTEST!

→ FRIDAY, SEPTEMBER 30TH
7:00 P.M.
FOOTHILLS MALL

BRING YOUR FRIENDS AND FAMILY TO
THE DANA ELEMENTARY ART SHOW!

This year's theme is Pop Art. Winners will be chosen by a
panel of professional artists and 1st place will win a
MYSTERY PRIZE.

ANOTHER DEAD END

After school I got out my art stuff to try something new, but I just arranged and rearranged it in the box:

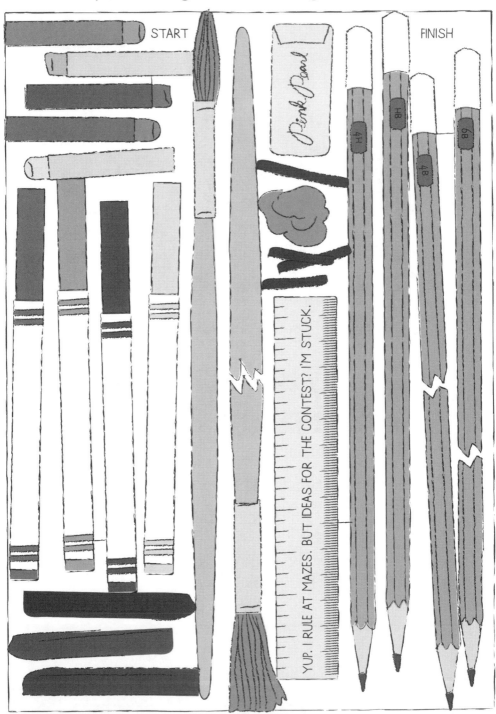

START

FINISH

YUP. I RULE AT MAZES. BUT IDEAS FOR THE CONTEST? I'M STUCK.

DUNGEONS & DRAGONS

I went with Jack to Dungeons & Dragons tonight. In case you didn't know, D&D is this uber-complicated game where you're a medieval character and you roll a bunch of weird dice and have pretend missions and battles and stuff.

Tommy Geller's older brother, Dagan, is the Dungeon Master. That means he's like the D&D coach. He helped me fill out a character sheet. I rolled the dice and ended up being a dwarf with swimming skills who's also a baker.

Tommy was there too. "So what are you working on for the art contest?" he asked me.

"How do you know about the contest?" I asked apprehensively.

"Jack said something about it last week. You're the best drawer I know. You're gonna win."

I'm the best drawer he knows? Remember, this is the same Tommy Geller who teased me about my unicorn drawing in front of the entire school a couple years ago. The same Tommy Geller who used to call me M.G. (short for Mighty Geek) because I like to draw.

I shrugged and admitted, "I can't think of anything good to make." Meanwhile, Jack rolled a 12-sided die* and cheered because he'd defeated the invisible orcs. (By the way, in D&D Jack is a an elf blacksmith who defends dwarves.)

A SHAPE WITH 12 SIDES LIKE THIS DIE IS CALLED A DODECAHEDRON.*

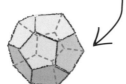

AND HERE'S WHAT IT WOULD LOOK LIKE ALL FLATTENED OUT. COOL, HUH?

"The subject is supposed to be something basic, something everyone knows about from everyday life, right?" said Tommy.

"Yeah."

"Well just pick the most basic thing you can think of and draw it, then color it in weird colors."

That helps...not at all, I thought.

And yeah. The D&D guys named me Adomorn Wyrmsbane. Jack is Jamian Moonshadow. And Tommy Geller is Lord Thoven Fletcher the Barbarian and also, apparently, an art appreciator. I'm pretty sure that's what Mr. Mot would call an interesting dichotomy.*

THE HUE IS QUITE STRIKING. AND WHAT A HARMONIOUS COMPOSITION!

CONTEST IDEA #4:
DROWNING JACK

Some uber-famous pop-art comes from comics, which is cool. There's one of a lady called "Drowning Girl," only it just looks like she's swimming and crying at the same time. What's the big deal?

Anyway, it made me think about Jack and how we play swimming games at our neighborhood pool in the summer and how Jack must feel when I always beat him at who-can-lie-on-the-hot-cement-the-longest.

So now I have four pop-art ideas for the contest. Meh. They're all just OK.

PASS INCOMPLETE

For homework tonight I had to practice my lines for the Shakespeare thing. Our class is going to perform the play for the first graders. It's not that big of a deal, but Mr. Krug said we should know our parts kinda well, so we don't just stand there reading like robots.

The assignment was to practice with someone in my family...but there was no <u>way</u> I was going to read a lovey-dovey play with my mom, and Dad is away on a business trip, so that left Timothy. And guess what Timothy was busy doing? Playing Just Dance 2 on the Wii in the family room...with Sasha! First the swinging, now the dancing. What's next? The holding hands? *Sick.* I just baby-barfed thinking about it.

Finally Sasha left and Timothy agreed to practice the play with me—if I would play catch with him.

So we took my Shakespeare book into the back yard, and we handed it back and forth as we read the stupid lines, like, "I have a great desire to eat a bottle of hay."

Every few minutes Timothy made me hike the ball to him then run to catch a pass.

Finally, after I'd run farther and dropped more passes than humanly possible, I collapsed onto the ground and refused to get up. Timothy brought out Gatorades from the house, and we lay on our backs in the grass, watching the first stars prick the dusky* sky.

"Remember when Mom used to sing 'Twinkle, Twinkle' to us?" asked Timothy.

"Yeah," I said. "Remember when we didn't need to know that Shakespeare existed?"

"Yeah. Remember when you could catch a football?"

"No. Remember when you didn't hang out with girls?"

"No. Plus Sasha's cute."

"So what?"

"Sew buttons on your underwear!" And he rolled me over and gave me a king-sized wedgie.

Shakespeare and football. I'm not sure they're the best combination.

BELLY-DOWN VIEW:

I TOLD TIMOTHY THAT THIS IS NOT WHAT THEY MEAN BY "TIGHT END."

THROW IT OUT THE WINDOW
(or, Defenestrate* It)

After school today I walked to Goosy's to talk to her about the art contest. She was in her studio, working on a sculpture. Goosy's a grandma, but she's also an artist. And a motorcycler. And a breakdancer. And lots of other ungrandma-like stuff.

"I've tried 4 different things, but I'm not coming up with anything good for the contest!" I

yelled up to her. She was hanging off a ladder, chipping away at a giant chunk of rock.

"Hmm," she said, climbing down and sitting with me at the studio's snack table. "Sometimes when I make something I don't like that much, I set it aside, because I might figure out a way to work with it some more and make it better. But sometimes I just toss things immediately."

"You mean you throw them away?"

"Darn tootin.' I'll show you."

IT'S VERY REWARDING TO SEE YOUR IDEAS TAKE FLIGHT—ONE WAY OR ANOTHER!

DOH!

Goosy walked me over to a window in her studio. She flung it open, and we peered over the sill, onto the ground below. There, behind a big bush, lay a mashed-up pile of paper, canvas, pottery, and other artsy stuff.

"I listen to my gut," she said. "If it tells me, 'This piece doesn't make you happy,' I just throw it away and start over."

"But why throw it out the <u>window?</u>"

"Because it feels good to throw something out a window once in a while, don't you think?"

"But you put so much work into your art!"

LOOKS LIKE IT'S ABOUT TIME FOR ANOTHER CLEAN-UP.

"Of course. Except I don't think of it as work. Life is mostly in the doing, anyway, not in the having. Besides, not everything we do in life deserves to be on display, Aldo. Most things are destined for the junk pile."

So I went home and did something that felt pretty audacious. I climbed the stairs to my bedroom, and I took the 4 art contest pieces I'd made so far, and yup, I hurled them out my window. Mr. Mot was riding by on his bike just in time to see everything fly through the air. He stopped and looked up at me.

"What say you, good Bottom?" he called.

"Just getting rid of some dud* art!" I yelled back to him.

"Thou art as wise as thou art beautiful!" he replied, loudly enough for all the neighbors to hear.

He was quoting from the Shakespeare play. It sounds even <u>more</u> dorky* in normal life.

DUNGEON DODGEBALL

BAP!

HEY!

If you know anything about me at all by now, you know that P.E. is my unfavoritest subject. Getting tired and sweaty is about as fun as...hmmm, let's see...having your soul sucked out of you by Dementors.* (Actually, whenever Harry's face is getting hoovered, I think: Presidential Physical Fitness Awards testing.)

But even I enjoy a good game of dodgeball.

Today our gym teacher, Mrs. Dalloway, said we were acting squirrelly and needed to dissipate* some of our energy. So she got out the dodgeball balls, lined them up down the middle of the gym, and blew the whistle. Since I'm not the fastest, I've gotta be the smartest. I let the quick kids run to grab the balls while I hang back and wait for one to be thrown at me.

Now that Bee's coming to Dana for P.E., she's one of the fast kids. She was on the opposite team today, and for some reason I have no clue about, she was bound and determined* to demolish* me.

PREPARE TO GET CLEANED, VACUUM-HATER.

In place of Bee's usual smile were the tight lips of anger. (I know those lips. My mom wears them a lot.) Bee grabbed a ball and fired it straight at me. It was a real doozy.* Sheesh. For someone who eats mostly vegetables, she's powerful!

I managed to dodge her first throw, but a few seconds later she hurled a second ball in my direction. It was coming too fast to get out of the way this time. I'd have to catch it. So I squared myself to the throw and got into catching position...but I timed my grabbing motion wrong and ended up in the dungeon. Dag nab it.

A minute later I was back on the court when I noticed out of the corner of my face that Danny, who was on my team, was running and throwing and dodging like a whirling dervish.* Man that kid can play dodgeball.

88

He crossed in front of me to snatch a ball that was dribbling* toward him across the center line.

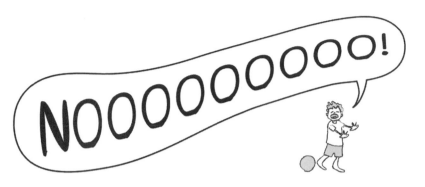

NOOOOOOOOO!

As he bent down to grab it, he didn't see the ball that Marvin Shoemaker (a.k.a. The Destroyer*) had thrown at him from a distance. The ball was heading straight for Danny!

"Heads up, Danny!" I yelled instinctively. But that didn't work, of course, so...I shoved him aside. The ball missed him, but he fell to the ground. Then he jumped to his feet and shoved me back. <u>Hard</u>. Now it was my turn to topple. Just as I fell, a ball bounced off my face. <u>Hard</u>. I'm pretty sure it was Bee.

All of this happened in a split second. Mrs. Dalloway blew her whistle. Danny's interpreter ran up and started translating Danny's furious signs.

"He pushed me first!" said Danny.

"But a ball was coming straight at him! I was just trying to move him out of the way!"

"I don't need your help!"

"You broke my finger!" My left pinkie finger was throbbing, and I could feel the high-pressure, watery feeling behind my eyeballs that means an embarrassing leakage is about to occur. "I'm going to the nurse's office!" I said. And I stormed off without looking back.

"You've been coming to see me an awful lot lately, Zelnick," said Nurse Dolores while she examined my hand.

"It's been a rough school year. And it's still the first month."

Nurse Dolores said my pinkie might be sprained. She taped it up and sent me back to class.

IN FACT, MOST PEOPLE WITH THIS TYPE OF INJURY GO ON TO LEAD PERFECTLY NORMAL LIVES.

NOW STOP DAWDLING,* ZELNICK.

Geez. Being a 5th grader is no walk in the park.

DEVIOUSNESS*

After school today, I snuck into Ms. Munroe's classroom for two sneaky reasons:

1. To leave a treat for Danny

    I put a Dora the Explorer coloring book on his desk with his name displayed on the cover. I even colored one of the pages for him with my jumbo crayons—outside the lines. Heh.

2. To open the mystery prize

    If the mystery prize was dumb, I figured, I'd just quit trying to come up with something good enough to win the art contest. (There's an I in quitter, did you notice?) But that meant I needed to know for sure what the prize is. I mean, you don't want to be giving up a solid gold brick or something really good.

On Ms. Munroe's desk sat a small, framed picture of her and some guy with red hair. Must be her brother. I slid open her desk drawer, and there was the package in all

its mysteriousness. I picked it up and carefully lifted up a corner of the tape. It lifted without tearing the paper! Yes! I could unwrap it, peek at the prize, then rewrap it...and no one would even notice!

I was just starting to peel back the bottom of the wrapping when I heard voices approaching the classroom door. I dropped the box back into the desk drawer, closed it, and dove under the desk.

In walked Ms. Munroe and Danny's interpreter. Even though my heart was pounding so hard I could hardly hear, I knew it was them because I recognized their voices. But I could also see their shoes. There were 3 pairs of shoes. And one of them belonged to <u>Danny</u>.

Danny, your painting is divine!*"gushed Ms. Munroe.

"Thanks. I just wanted to ask you if I should work on the color some more," said the interpreter for Danny. "Is there too much blue? Or do you think it needs more orange?"

He said he was painting a buck. *He made a blue and orange deer?* That's weird. I tried peering out a crack in the side of the desk, but I couldn't see it.

"Hmmm....," she said. "Since this is in the style of Jasper Johns, I think he might have added even more blue. But this is your work, so you should decide on the color balance that feels right to you."

"I think more orange," said Danny through the interpreter.

"More orange it is!" said Ms. Munroe. "Have a good weekend. And don't forget your coloring book!"

There was a shuffling of feet in the room as she handed him Dora. No more words were spoken, but Danny chortled as the three of them walked out of the room. When he laughs, I've noticed, he sounds pretty much like any other kid.

Whew. I hadn't been caught! I had a leg cramp from crouching, and I banged my head against the top of the desk as I stood, though. I was headed toward the door when Ms. Munroe came waltzing back into the art room. (Well, she doesn't really waltz so much as stumble.)

"Aldo! Can I help you with something?" she said.

And it happened <u>again</u>! I was voiceless. I was holding my sore head and my leg hurt and I couldn't speak, and life just doesn't get any more demoralizing* than that. All I could do was shake my head no and limp away down the hall, feeling (a) relieved not to be caught and (b) dumber than a box of Jack's rocks.*

EXCUSE ME?! THESE ROCKS ARE <u>NOT</u> DUMB. <u>NO</u> ROCKS ARE DUMB!

DITTO.*

ALL MIXED UP

After P.E. today, Danny handed me a note:

I was kinda scared, but also kinda curious. Like you feel when you have the urge to sneak down into your grandma's dark, cobwebby basement, just to see what's down there. So I went to my locker, and Danny was there waiting for me. His interpreter was nowhere in sight. This was gonna be awkward.

It was lunch period, and the hallway was a ghost town. Danny flashed me one of his bogus charismatic smiles, but then he grabbed my shirt and started yanking me down the hall!

"Hey! Ouch! Don't hurt me!" I said, but he just tugged and looked straight ahead. His long hair was making him look very evil all of a sudden.

I'M SORRY I PUSHED YOU! I'LL GIVE YOU MY LITTLE DEBBIES! I HAVE A WHOLE BOX IN MY LOCKER...

I was about to throw myself to the ground—figuring I was too heavy for him to drag—when he stopped in front of an art contest poster. It was the one Ms. Munroe had made. (I drew it on page 69. Did you notice its discombobulation?*)

Danny pulled a little pad of paper out of his pocket and wrote quickly: "We should fix."

"What? Why?" I asked. "Because there are a few little mistakes?"

Danny rolled his eyes at me. "Ms. Munroe isn't dumb," he wrote. "Dyslexic.* And clumsy."

"Ohhhh," I said, wondering if he could lip-read all those extra Hs. "How did you figure it out?"

"She writes class notes for me," he scribbled. "She mixes up letters." He pointed down the hallway and started to speak in sign language, then shook his head in frustration and started to write again: "Art room. We'll get orange paint and fix."

"We can't just break into the art room," I said. (Yes, I am aware of the duplicity* of this statement.)

"We can," he said-wrote. "We're 5th."

He had a point. And it was for a good cause. "OK. Let's hurry."

99

So we ran to the art room, got a Dixie cup of orange paint and a small brush, and ran back to the poster. Miraculously, no teachers saw us. We fixed the spelling mistakes the best we could, then we tossed the paint and brush into the nearest trash can. Just as we finished, the bell rang.

I'd missed lunch!

Sigh. My dad always says I'm the kind of kid who never misses a meal. If only he were right.

MY BIOLOGICAL CLOCK

THE MAN BEHIND THE MASK

Today we had a dress rehearsal for the dumb Shakespeare play. And guess what I get to wear. On my head.

Remember my character, Nick Bottom, who starts out as your basic weaver guy? Welp, as the play goes on, he turns out to be more and more of a dolt.* In fact, he's so ridiculous that his head turns into a donkey and he doesn't even realize it. (You'd have to be pretty dumb to have something besides hair on your dome* and not even know it.)

Then, even though Bottom's a donkey, Queen Titania falls in love with him because Oberon, Titania's husband, squirted magic juice into her eyes when she was sleeping. Titania wakes up and sees Bottom.

Mr. Mot said that Titania is <u>supposed</u> to kiss Bottom a bunch of times, but if she makes lovey-dovey expressions, that's enough for 5th grade. After that I was <u>glad</u> I could hide my real face inside of a giant donkey mask.

PERCHANCE TO DREAM

I just woke up from the best dream ever.

I was Bottom the donkey, but instead of being a dunderhead, I was a ninja-donkey. I talked in wise sayings, and when bad guys came along, I flipped and kicked and spun like a tornado with hooves.

Everyone bowed down to me and brought me gifts of special foods and riches. Like, one guy gave me a sausage-and-onion deep-dish pizza in the shape of a giant trumpet (NOT a flute). And another guy came bearing video game controllers made of the finest chocolate. When they started to melt, you just ate them!

Jack was Oberon, king of the fairies, just like in the Shakespeare play, only he was dressed as his D&D character—an elf blacksmith and defender of dwarves. (You could tell because he had pointy ears, a blacksmith's hammer, and a bunch of short guys with red beards lined up behind him.) Bacon Boy was one of Oberon's fairies. He wore wings instead of a blue cape.

Bee was a bee. She came floating into town on a magic carpet made of flower petals. Danny rode alongside her on a jet-powered skateboard. They skidded to a stop in front of me and challenged me to a drawing contest.

The crowd gasped, because no one dares to diss* ninja-donkeys. But the three of us started drawing, and we drew so fast that sparks flew from our pencil-tips. Seconds later, when the drawings were finished, we turned our easels toward the crowd. Everyone went wild—whistling and yelling and rushing up to me in a frenzy. They hoisted me to their shoulders and carried me down a street paved with Dots candy.

Now if only I could remember what I drew, because I still need an idea for the art contest, and obviously this one was a real crowd-pleaser.

ADOMORN! ADOMORN!
ADOMORN!
ADOMORN! ADOMORN!
ADOMORN!
I CAME. I DREW. I CONQUERED.
ADOMORN!
ADOMORN! ADOMORN!
ADOMORN! ADOMORN!

TO TELL
THE TRUTH

I went to the fort to chillax after school today, and after a little bit Bee and Jack showed up too.

"I'm sorry I hit you in the face with that dodgeball," said Bee.

"Sorry I said your vacuum cleaner is dumb," I mumbled. (*Even though it is kinda dumb*, I thought but didn't say out loud this time.)

"I'm over it," said Bee. "Besides, I came up with something better than a vacuum."

I rolled off the fort futon, face-down onto the pine-needled dirt. "Ugh! I still don't have a good idea!" I moaned as I beat my fists against the ground. "I don't know what to make!"

"Dude, the contest is in 2 days," said Jack.

"I know! And I uh...happened to hear Danny talking to Ms. Munroe about his painting. It sounds really cool. Maybe even good enough to win. Ugh! I can't work under this pressure!"

"School is harder this year," admitted Jack. "That lakes of the world test this week kicked my derrière.*"

Bee just rolled her eyes at us. I bet she knows every lake in the universe.

"5th grade is the worst!" I realized.
"Remember how awesome it was to be a little
kid?"

"1st grade was probably as good as it gets,"
sighed Jack.

"Plus, I keep getting sick this year!" I said.
"I can't talk, I feel dizzy, my stomach hurts. I'm
practically best friends with Nurse Dolores these
days. I think I have a brain tumor."

"But you don't feel sick all the time, right?" said Bee.

"No, just sometimes."

"Like Tuesdays and Thursdays at 8:30 in the morning."

"Hey, that's when we have art!" said Jack.

"Exactly," said Bee. "Aldo, are you so dense* that you don't even know what's wrong with you?"

I couldn't tell where she was headed with this, but I didn't like the sound of it. I shook my head and scowled at her.

She giggled, then she sighed. "The only kind of sick you are is lovesick, you dimwit.* You have a crush on Ms. Munroe!"

"Ew. You like Ms. Munroe? That's disgusting," said Jack. "I mean, I like Ms. Munroe too, but you like her?"

I could feel my brain start to vibrate. It was getting ready to explode for the second time in a month.

"No! I do not!" I said. "That's easily the dumbest thing I've ever heard." And once again I crawled out from under the fort tree and left my so-called friends to their asinine behavior.

THIS IS SO...STUPID.
THIS IS SO...OUTRAGEOUS.
THIS IS SO...IDIOTIC.
THIS IS SO...PREPOSTEROUS.
THIS IS SO...LUDICROUS.
THIS IS SO...BIZARRE.
THIS IS SO...MENTAL.
THIS IS SO...BONKERS.
THIS IS SO...RIDICULOUS.
THIS IS SO...NUTTY.
THIS IS SO...DAFFY.*
THIS IS SO DUMB!

10 Ways to Tell You're in Like

Written by: 🐝   To be filled out by: Aldo

1. You shower and comb your hair.   T or (F)   HA. NOT DOING THAT.

2. You pick out your clothes carefully so you look nice.   T or (F)   NOPE. WHEW.

3. You don't know what to say when you're around the person, or you have problems talking.   (T) or F

4. You smile like a doofus.   (T) or F   OH GEEZ.

5. Your stomach feels throw-uppish.   (T) or F

6. You pay attention to details about the person. (T) or F LIKE HER HANDS.

7. You notice what the person's voice is like. (T) or F BUTTER BRICKLE ICE CREAM! (HOW COULD YOU NOT NOTICE?!)

8. You do nice things for the person. (T) or F DOES PICKING UP BOOKS AND MAKING POSTERS COUNT?

9. You get goose-bumpy if the person touches you. (T) or F OH NO.

10. You think something might be wrong with you. (T) or F THIS IS NOT GOOD.

If you've circled True for 7 or more, you're definitely in like. If you've circled True for all 10...it's love!

ALL THE WORLD'S
A STAGE

Today was our performance of *A Midsummer Night's Dream*.

It was in the school library, and Mrs. Muñoz's 1st graders all sat criss-cross applesauce on the floor to be our audience. A few parents and teachers came to watch too. They stood around the edges of the room and gave us kids the universal grown-up encouragement signs: smiling and nodding and clapping. And Mr. Mot was there, of course, in his funny hat and tights. He was director and narrator.

I was actually having a good time being Bottom! He's a funny character, and I got to say some lines that were making all the kids and grown-ups crack up.

The play is done in 5 short acts. Act 1 and Act 2 went well. But then in the middle of Act 3, I saw Ms. Munroe slip through the doorway at the back of the library. She stopped to watch along with the rest of the grown-ups.

At that point, Mr. Mot was narrating. "But Puck has put a spell on Bottom," he said.

This is the part in the play where Bottom turns into a donkey. So I put on my donkey mask—which made all the 1st graders practically die laughing—but then I couldn't deliver my next line! Instead, I just stood there while Mr. Mot stage-whispered to me: "If I were fair, Thisby, I were only thine!"

He thought I'd forgotten what I was supposed to say, but that wasn't the problem at all. I <u>remembered</u> my line, but I couldn't <u>say</u> it. I couldn't say <u>anything</u>.

Donkey-headed and sweaty, I ran from the library. Mr. Krug followed me down the hallway.

"Aldo, are you OK?"

I took off my mask and threw it to him. "I don't feel good," I said.

"You don't look good," he said. "Why don't you go to the nurse's office. Maybe you're coming down with someth—"

"Gotta go," I interrupted, and I ran-walked to the bathroom, where my problem took the form of explosive gastrointestinal distress.*

UM, YEAH. YOU MIGHT WANT TO GIVE IT A MINUTE.

I'm coming down with something all right, I thought. A case of ridiculousness. A case of dumbness to the 10th degree. I'm afraid Bee was right. I'm having Ms. Munroe-related issues. If this is what it's going to be like to be a big kid, I'm gonna stay a little kid forever. Like Peter Pan. Or Dennis the Menace. Or Calvin.

When I got to the nurse's office, 3 4th grade boys were there too.

"Lemme guess... something's wrong with your throat," said Nurse Dolores.

I nodded.

"These boys had art class last period and now they can't talk, either," she said. "Do you think it could be fumes from the paints the new art teacher is using this year?"

I looked at the 3 boys sitting there. So young, so clueless, so miserable. "I think it's definitely something about that new art teacher," I said, "something devastating.*"

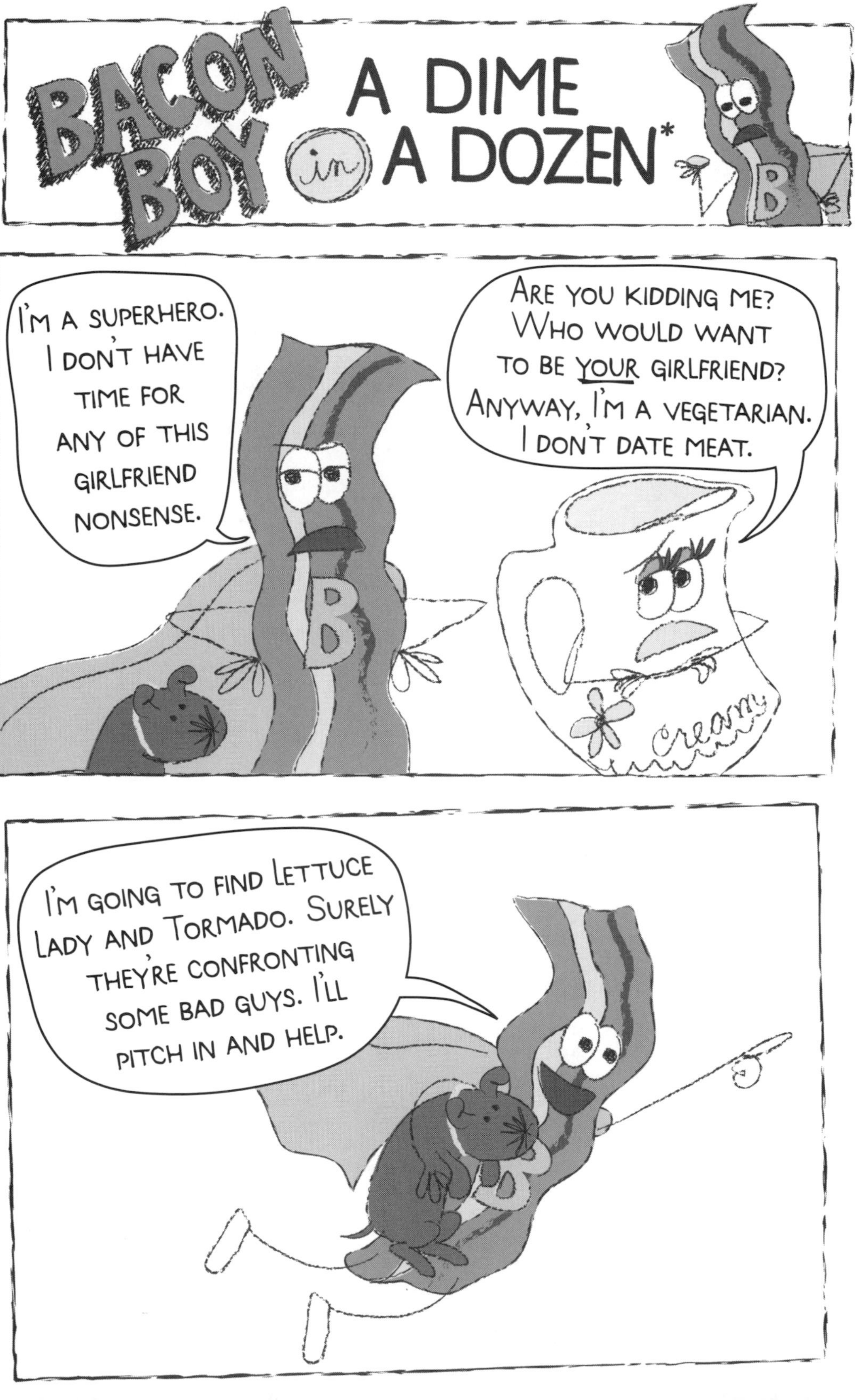
BACON BOY in A DIME A DOZEN*
I'M A SUPERHERO. I DON'T HAVE TIME FOR ANY OF THIS GIRLFRIEND NONSENSE.
ARE YOU KIDDING ME? WHO WOULD WANT TO BE YOUR GIRLFRIEND? ANYWAY, I'M A VEGETARIAN. I DON'T DATE MEAT.
creamy
I'M GOING TO FIND LETTUCE LADY AND TORMADO. SURELY THEY'RE CONFRONTING SOME BAD GUYS. I'LL PITCH IN AND HELP.

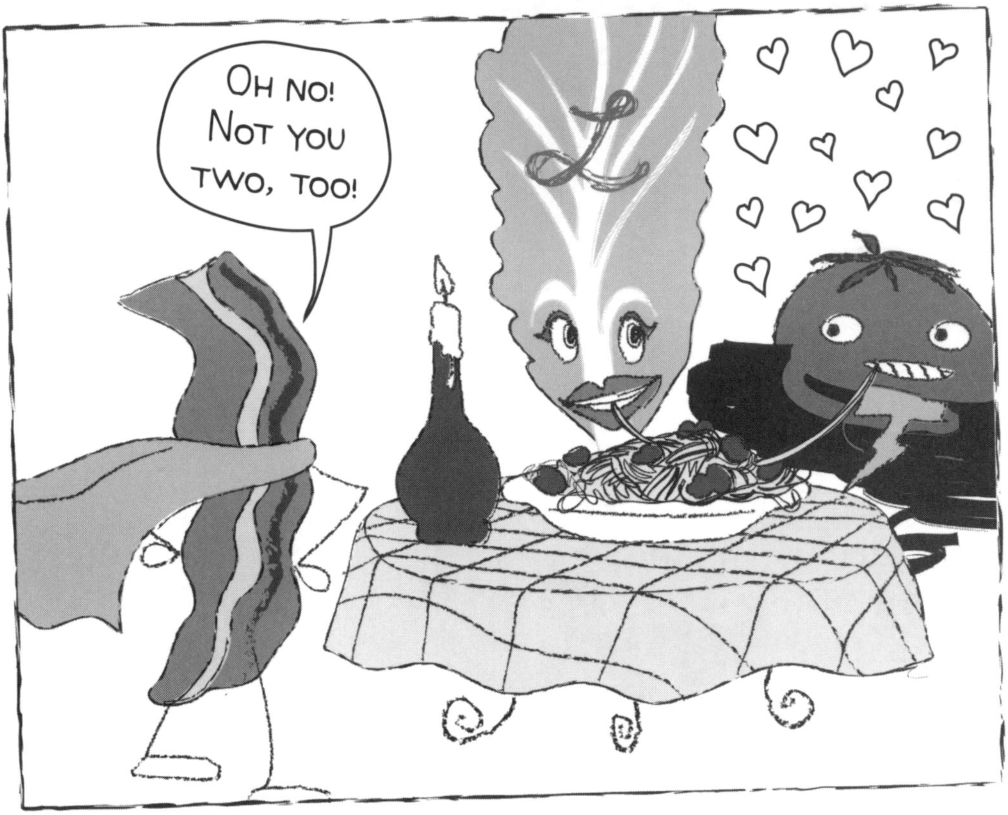
OH NO!
NOT YOU
TWO, TOO!

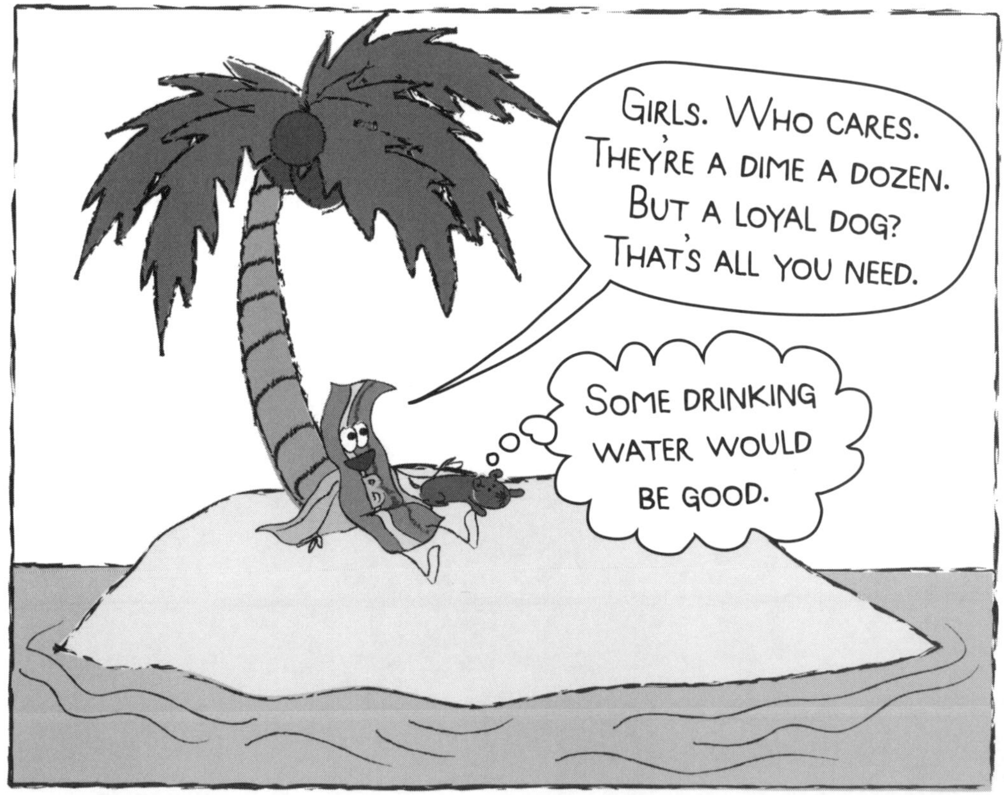
GIRLS. WHO CARES.
THEY'RE A DIME A DOZEN.
BUT A LOYAL DOG?
THAT'S ALL YOU NEED.
SOME DRINKING
WATER WOULD
BE GOOD.

JUST DUNK IT

I have informed my parents that they will be homeschooling me from now on.

I will not be returning to Dana Elementary— or to any public place, for that matter.

I have locked myself up in my room, where I will live out the remainder of my days in the doldrums* of solitude and hunger.

Wait. I smell cookies. BRB.

So, I followed the smell down to the kitchen where, sure enough, Dad was just pulling a warm pan of snickerdoodles from the oven. He patted a stool and poured me a tall glass of milk. Mr. Mot must have smelled the cookies, too, because he rang the doorbell about then and joined us at the kitchen counter.

"You played a good part, Aldo," said Mr.
Mot, dunking his cookie. "Bottom is a memorable
character."

"I stunk," I said. "Did you forget that I ran
off during the middle of the play?"

"No, I did not forget," he said. "But you had
many fine moments in Acts 1 and 2. And I took
over the part of Bottom after you left. After all,

the show must go on—even if the lovely new art teacher enters the room."

I could feel my cheeks get cherry-slushie red, but I kept my eyes on my cookie as it plunged into my glass of milk. My pinkie finger on my dunking hand was still sore from the dodgeball incident, but I carried on.

"Ohhh! So there's the rub!" said Dad. "Aldo came home from school insisting that he be homeschooled from now on. Now I understand."

"Ah, young love," said Mr. Mot. "Equal parts delicious delirium* and dreadful devastation. When I was a young Don Juan,* in the navy, I carried a torch for a lovely librarian in every port."

"My first crush was my best friend's big sister," said my dad. "Debbie Dixon. A cheerleader. I made a fool of myself whenever she was around."

"Did you talk to her?" I asked.

"Oh, I don't remember trying to talk," said Dad. "I just remember pulling her ponytail and showing her how many push-ups I could do."

"I can't talk when Ms. Munroe's around," I said. "It's so dumb!"

"Dumb indeed," said Mr. Mot. "You're dumbstruck.*"

"What does that mean?"

"It means you lost the ability to speak. You were speechless. Tongue-tied. Mute. Dumb."

"Dumb means you can't talk?"

"That's one of the word's meanings."

"That's dumb," I said.

We sat in silence for a while, dunking and munching. I thought about everything that had been happening this crazy month and how glad I would be when all the newness of 5th grade wasn't so new and distracting* anymore. Like Ms. Munroe. And band. And Danny.

"So Danny can't talk," I said. "Is he dumbstruck?"

"No," said Dad. "He's not speechless...he speaks with his hands."

"But you know," said Mr. Mot, "language is always changing. We don't use many of Shakespeare's words these days, do we? A long time ago we used to call people who couldn't hear or talk 'deaf and dumb.' The problem is, the word 'dumb' has two meanings—one of them not so nice. So, we don't call deaf people 'dumb' anymore. Even though you <u>were</u> dumb for a time today, my young friend."

"You can say that again," I muttered.

Dad and Mr. Mot chuckled and slapped me on the back then, cuz that's what guys do at the end of a macho conversation like the one we just had.

CONTEST IDEA #5: IT'S A SECRET

OK. Everything that happened today finally gave me an idea for the art contest. Which is tomorrow!!!

I needed to ask Danny something first, though, so my dad helped me figure out how to call his house. I talked to his mom, and she said Danny could text with me on his cell phone. So I borrowed Dad's cell phone, and I texted him my question. He texted me his answer. Just like that.

I'm going to get to work on my contest entry now. It's last-minute, but I feel good about it. Really good.

GRAND CHAMPION

Welp, tonight was the big night. The Dana Elementary art show and contest.

Everybody and their brother were at the mall. I mean, I was there, and so were Timothy and my parents and Goosy and Mr. Mot. Bee and Jack and their families. Danny and his parents and a bunch of their sign-speaking friends. Bazillions of other kids from our school and their families. Tommy and Dagan Geller. Ms. Munroe and the guy from the picture on her desk. Her brother or whoever.

Without further ado, here's what happened:

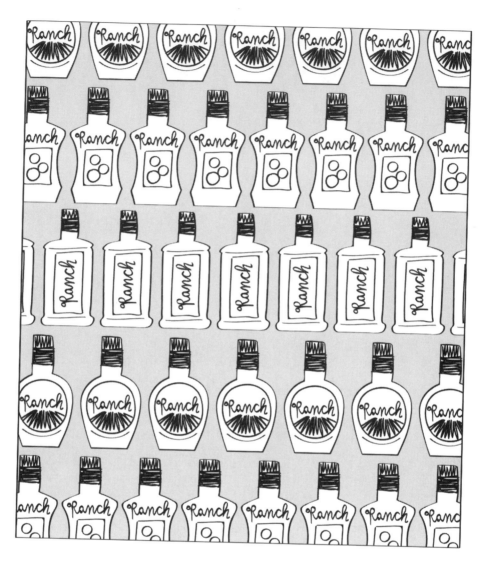

Bee made this amazing drawing of rows
and rows of salad dressing. She said that ranch
dressing is popular with kids...and that that's a
good thing because it helps make vegetables more
popular with kids. (I beg to differ, but...)

Danny's painting wasn't of a deer...it was of a dollar bill! THAT kind of buck! He didn't make it green, though, he made it orange and blue, just like I overheard.

Daniel D. Peterson

⌐ This was my painting. I kept thinking about
how Danny said he hoped the mystery gift wasn't
an iPod. Most kids would go crazy for the latest
generation. iPods are uber-popular, and I've seen
the old pop-artish ads about them, which made me
wonder even more if Danny knows what music
is. So I texted him to ask. As it turns out, you
can love music even if you can't hear it with your
ears! I decided my painting could show all the things
Danny told me music means to him.

So, I thought for sure Bee or Danny was going to win the art contest. I mean, mine was pretty good, and theirs were bodacious... But guess who won? Jack!

I didn't even consider Jack.

He made a mosaic of Jim Morrison (Jack said he was some famous singer in a band called The Doors) out of tiny pieces of rock. He glued little stones next to each other on top of a big photo of Jim's face. It was kinda like a paint-by-number, only it was a rock-by-number.

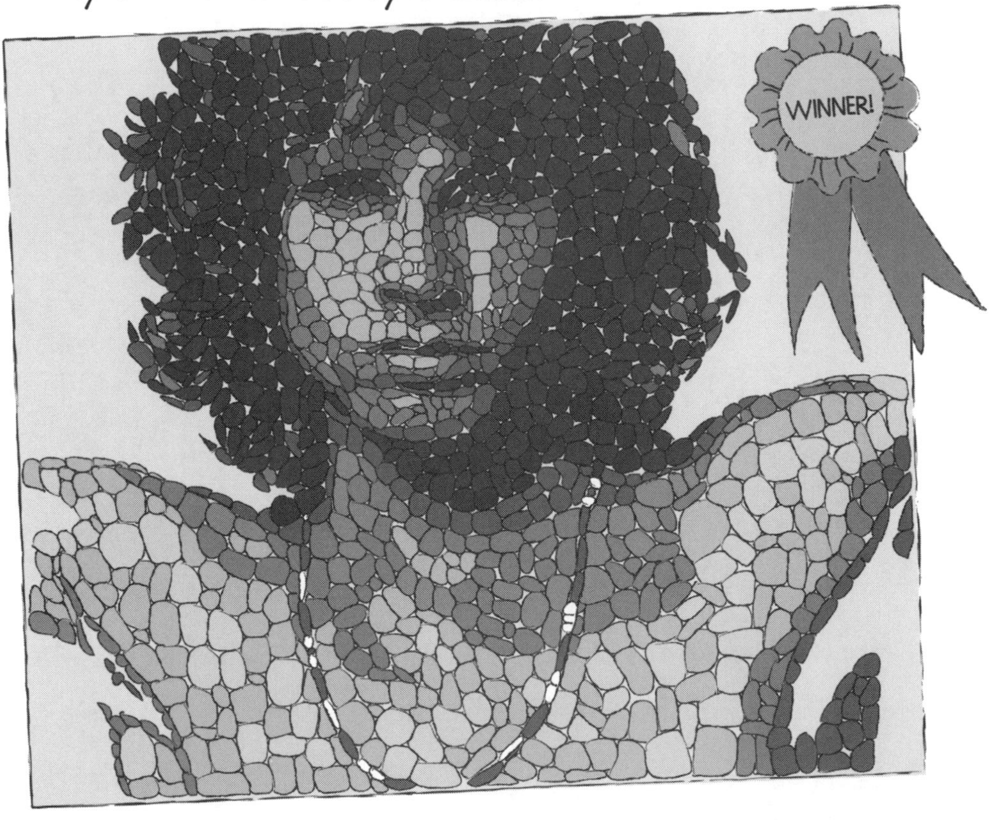
WINNER!

"What?" he asked when I stood in front of his piece with my mouth agape. "The assignment was to show something popular. I like rocks, but they're not that popular. But rock <u>stars</u>...they're popular. So it's a rock star. Get it?"

Everyone crowded around and clapped as Ms. Munroe stuck the big blue ribbon on Jack's mosaic and handed him the mystery gift. He tore off the wrapping paper, opened the box, and lifted out...a little sculpture of a yellow and purple hand.

"Wow...it's phrygian marble, from Turkey!" said Jack, and he hugged that hand to his chest like it was the most special gift anyone had ever given him.

Goosy nudged me. "I made that and donated it for the contest," she whispered. "It's a small-scale model of the big sculpture I'm making in my studio right now. It's American Sign Language for 'I love you,' which I do." And she gave me a gigantic Goosy hug and kiss, right there in the mall, in front of everyone. Sheesh.

So the mystery prize turned out to be a dud. I was glad I didn't have to stand there in front of everyone pretending to be excited about a hand made of rock, and Jack looked so happy that I felt a bubble of happiness for him. But I <u>was also</u> bummed that I didn't win.

Ms. Munroe and some guy walked over to me then. It was the guy with the red hair from the picture on her desk. They were holding hands.

"Aldo, I'd like you to meet my fiancé, Arthur," she said. "Arthur, this is one of my most exceptional students."

I nodded and looked at my shoes.

YOU REALLY KNOW YOUR WAY AROUND A CANVAS, MY FRIEND.

"Sweet painting," Arthur said to me. "Marilyn's told me all about you."

Marilyn?

"Uh, thanks," I managed.

"The subject you chose for your painting was truly inspiring, Aldo," said Ms. Munroe. "I'm proud of you." And she reached out to shake my hand.

As my smaller hand was covered up by her bigger one, I felt a shift inside me, like a coin flipping to its other side. Ms. Munroe was <u>proud</u> of me. Like my mom and dad and Goosy and Mr. Mot are proud of me. She was just another nice grown-up, and I was just a kid, and everything was the way it's supposed to be. <u>Mostly</u>.

"Just don't go sneaking into my desk anymore," she added mommishly before walking away. *Busted but not punished*, I thought. *Whew*.

My parents were treating me to a food court frozen yogurt when Danny and his parents came to say hello. "I like your painting," he signed and his mom interpreted. "Maybe I could buy it from you."

"Nah," I said. "You can have it."

"Do you want to trade? My painting for your painting?"

"Sure," I said. And that's how I ended up with the orange and blue dollar bill I'm looking at right now. I thumb-tacked it to the wall in my bedroom. I just noticed that he signed it like a big-time artist, in black marker in the bottom-right corner: Daniel D. Peterson. I wonder what the D stands for.

DAEDALUS? DAFFY?
DAHL? DAMIEN? DANTE? DARBY?
DARTAGNAN? DARWIN? DENETHOR?
DESLOGES? DEWEY? DIABLO? DIAPER? (I WISH.)
DINN? DILBERT? DISCO? DOBBY? DOLPH?
DONATELLO? DONOVAN? DOONESBURY?
DRACO?...

DENOUEMENT*

I'M INSULTED. I SOUND MUCH BETTER THAN THAT.

In band today, Marvin Shoemaker had a meltdown.

We were playing "Mary Had a Little Lamb." I'm starting to get the hang of the flute—blowing <u>across</u> the hole instead of into it and moving my fingers onto the right spots. Bee is a whiz on the drums, of course, and Jack loves his trombone almost as much as he loves his marble hand.

But poor Marvin. He can't seem to make his trumpet sound like anything but a dying cat. He was puffing his cheeks and getting red in the face, as usual. His eyeballs were practically popping out of his skull. You've got to give him credit. The kid tries.

Today he snapped, though. He dropped his trumpet to his lap and started to cry. Yes, he was actually bawling, right there in 5th grade band class.

And that's when I realized I had an opportunity to do something nice for a fellow human being.

I went to sit next to Marvin, and I put my arm around his shoulder. Mrs. Dulcet, seeing that Marvin was being tended to, smiled at me and kept the rest of the band playing so their eyes would be on their sheet music instead of on poor Marvin.

"Dude, you hate the trumpet, don't you," I said.

"Yes!" he sniveled. "But my parents are making me play it because my sister played it."

"I understand your pain. That's why I'm prepared to put you out of your misery. You can have my flute, and I'll take your trumpet. I know... the trumpet is more demanding,* and the flute is a much cooler instrument...but I'm willing to make that sacrifice for a good friend."

"Wow. You would do that?" asked Marvin. He didn't even dither.*

"Darn tootin'," I said.

And that's how I came to be Dana Elementary 5th grade band's newest Dizzy Gillespie.*

After band, it was lunchtime. Jack got to have the lunch of his choice with Ms. Munroe, in the art room. He invited me to join them, and I figured why not, I might get a few leftover french fries. So I brought my sack lunch up to the art room, and there were Ms. Munroe and Jack, dining on peanut butter sandwiches!

"You chose peanut butter sandwiches," I accused Jack.

"They're my favorite. I have them every single day for lunch."

"I know! But you could have had a bacon double-cheeseburger! Or chicken nuggets! Or deep-dish pizza!"

"You know how they say beauty is in the eye of the beholder?" asked Ms. Munroe, wiping the jelly she'd dribbled down the front of her shirt. "Well, taste is in the mouth of the eater, I guess."

Ms. MUNROE MADE THESE PBJs EXTRA-SPECIAL. SHE USED D'ANJOU PEAR* PRESERVES INSTEAD OF GRAPE JELLY.

By the way, Danny told me his middle name is Danger. He's quite the comedian. And today when I got home from school, guess what I found in my backpack:

The folder that Aldo told DANNY he really wants to marry because he LOVES it so much.

Ha-ha, very funny. So I've prepared something for Danny tomorrow. A nice yummy baggie of leftover deviled eggs* I found in the back of our refrigerator. They'll smell delightful by the time he discovers them in the bottom of <u>his</u> backpack.

SIGN LANGUAGE
ALPHABET

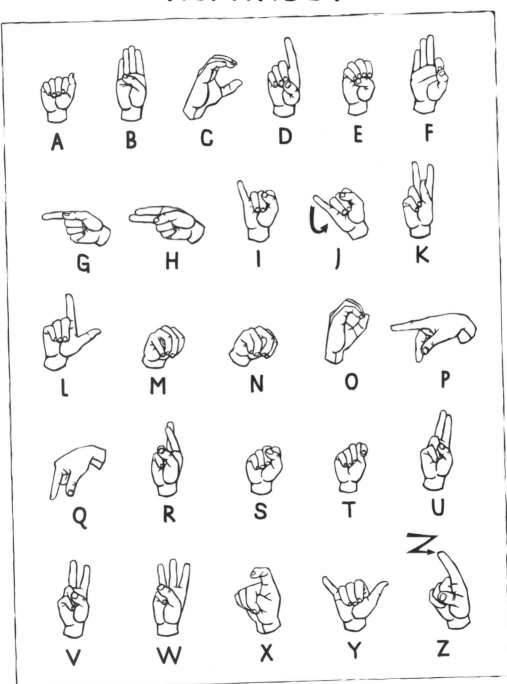

OTHER HANDY SIGNS

HORSE + SMALL = PONY!

BACON

DANNY MADE THIS ONE UP JUST FOR ME! COOL! (BUT WAIT! IS HE DISSING MY HAIR?)

ALDO

HANG ON A SECOND.

GO OUTSIDE.

WE ZELNICKS HAVE OUR OWN SIGN LANGUAGE TOO.

TAKE ME FOR A WALK.

"D" GALLERY

Mr. Mot used to be an English teacher. He's a word nerd, and he likes to help me use awesome words in my sketchbooks. I mark the best words with one of these: * (it's called an asterisk). When you see an * you'll know you can look here, in the Gallery, to see what the word means. If you don't know how to say some of the words, just ask Mr. Mot. Or someone you know who's like Mr. Mot. Or go to aldozelnick.com, and we'll say them for you.

daffy (pg. 111): dumb in a silly way. Like that old-time cartoon character Daffy Duck, who says "dethpicable!*"

Dagwood (pg. 45): I asked my dad what Dagwood means. It's some old-guy comic character.

d'anjou pear (pg. 139): a fancy French pear that tastes like a basic pear.

daikon radish (pg. 28): Proof of just how gross these giant white radishes are: "daikon" means "large root" in Japanese.

THEY'RE BASICALLY BIG ALBINO CARROTS. I'LL PASS.

dawdling (pg. 91): being slow and lazy on purpose. Also called dilly-dallying.

dastardly (pg. 19): sneaky and mean

debris (pg. 13): random, leftover junk. Pronounced duh•bree.

deceive (pg. 36): trick

Yo. It's NOT DAWDLING IF IT'S THE FASTEST YOU CAN GO.

OH WHAT A TANGLED WEB WE WEAVE.

(DID YOU KNOW THERE ARE 3 THINGS CALLED DADDY LONGLEGS? ONLY ONE IS A BONA FIDE SPIDER.)

decent (pg. 20): acceptable to Moms

deer in headlights (pg. 70): when you're surprised by something and have a frozen, stunned look on your face

defenestrate (pg. 82): to throw something out the window. Weird. So, are there separate words for all the places you can throw things? What's the word for "to throw something under your bed," for example? (My mom's word for this is: "pigsty.")

delectable (pg. 42): uber-yummy

delicacy (pg. 56): a food that's kind of rare AND delicious. But also possibly gross, like caviar (fish eggs), fern parts (called fiddleheads), and truffles (the mushroom kind, not the chocolate kind).

Delight, Turkish (pg. 56): the candy that Edmund loves so much that he betrays his brother and sisters to get it. Hm. I might betray Timothy for a platter of crispy bacon...

delirium (pg. 123): when real life feels like a dream

delusional (pg. 11): thinking so crazy and wrongly about something that you're basically making things up

demanding (pg. 137): difficult to do

Dementors (pg. 86): those creepy, floaty Grim Reaper-type guys in Harry Potter that suck your soul out of your face

demolish (pg. 87): to wreck and ruin

demoralizing (pg. 96): something that really takes away your enthusiasm and happiness

denouement (pg. 136): a Frenchy word that Mr. Mot taught me. Pronounced day•new•mah. It means the conclusion of a story—the boring part that's left after the exciting climax.

dense (pg. 110): stupidly unable to understand something

depressor, tongue (pg. 63): those extra-large wooden popsicle-sticks-without-the-yummy-popsicle they stick in your mouth at the doctor's office

derrière (pg. 108): fancy French word for butt. (Jack didn't actually say derrière. He said butt. I was just trying to be polite.)

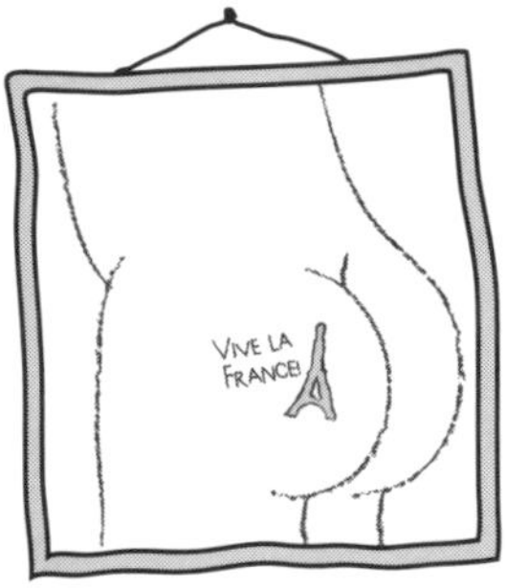
VIVE LA FRANCE!

dervish, whirling (pg. 88): OK, this is weird. A dervish is a Turkish monk. Sometimes dervishes do a dance where they spin around in circles. Somehow the phrase whirling dervish has come to mean somebody who's very fast and has lots of energy.

despair (pg. 20): deep sadness that seems like it will never end

dethspicable (actually - despicable) (pg. 143): mean and icky

destiny (pg. 59): what's going to happen to you, whether you like it or not

destroyer (pg. 89): someone who likes demolishing. Marvin's all tough in P.E., but he's a wimp in band, thank goodness.

determined (bound and) (pg. 87): This is a phrase that means you're not just determined—you're really determined.

detest (pg. 20): hate a lot

devastating (pg. 118): something that brings you to your knees it's so bad

deviled eggs (pg. 140): those kind of eggs that are hardboiled then cut in half, with some extra delicious stuff mixed together with the yolk. Yumbo.

deviousness (pg. 92): when you're being sneaky to gain an advantage

devise (pg. 18): think of a way to

dichotomy (pg. 77): when two things that are very different are put together

die (pg. 76): Two or more dice are called dice. One dice is called a die. Don't ask me why.

differ (beg to) (pg. 49): a fancier way of saying disagree

dig (pg. 7): a hippie word for "like," as in, "Do you dig doughnuts? I do!"

dime a dozen (pg. 119): common; easy to get

diminutive (pg. 50): teeny-tiny

dimwit (pg. 110): dumbhead

dinky (pg. 21): the same as diminutive but easier to say and spell

disapproval (pg. 68): The word-starter "dis" kinda means "opposite of." So disapproval means the opposite of approval. Not OK with.

disbelief (pg. 29): the opposite of belief; beyond dubiousness into definitely not believing

disco (pg. 32): My parents listen to this music from the 1970s sometimes and it makes them point their fingers up and down and shake their derrières. It's bewildering.

discombobulation (pg. 98): serious mixed-upedness

disgrace (pg. 20): the opposite of grace; shame

disgust (pg. 55): the opposite of gust. What? OK, some of these dis words don't work that way. Disgust means being mad and grossed out.

disparaging (pg. 72): making fun of in kind of a mean way

diss (pg. 105): slang for disrespect, which means to be rude to

dissipate (pg. 86): release; get rid of

distinct (pg. 66): sharp and clear

DISTOL (pg. 71): text-speak for, "Did I say that out loud?"

distracting (pg. 124): taking your concentration away from whatever it's supposed to be on

distress, gastrointestinal (pg. 117): Uh...so, this is a nice way of saying diarrhea. What?! I can't help it! It's what happens to me sometimes when I'm nervous!

JUST SAVING SOME FOR LATER!

dither (pg. 138): have a hard time deciding

ditto (pg. 96): "I agree" or "me, too."

divine (pg. 94): heavenly

Dizzy Gillespie (pg. 138): only the most famous trumpet player of all time

dodecahedron (pg. 76): a shape with 12 sides

doldrums (pg. 121): unhappy, depressing days

dolomite (pg 41): some kind of rock. I don't know. Ask Jack.

dolt (pg. 101): dumbhead

dome (pg. 101): head; noggin. Uh, I guess I had some stuff on my dome and didn't realize it. Heh.

Don Juan (pg. 123): I asked Mr. Mot about this one. He said Don Juan was a guy who had lots of girlfriends. Ick.

doodling (pg. 60): randomly drawing for no reason

doofus (pg. 29): dumbhead

dorky (pg. 85): embarrassingly uncool

doozy (pg. 87): something that's extraordinary

dopey (pg. 81): goofy-dumb

dread (pg. 20): scaredness that feels especially awful

dribbling (pg.89): rolling slowly; also means bouncing a basketball. Weird.

dubious (pg. 48): full of doubt and unsureness

dud (pg. 85): loserish

dumber than a box of rocks (pg. 96): This is a saying that means uber-dumb. Despite Jack's disapproval.

dumbstruck (pg. 124): when your brain gets struck with an idea or piece of information so surprising or confusing that you can't talk. You're literally speechless.

dunderhead (pg. 66): dumbhead

Dungeons & Dragons (pg. 52): a game where you pretend to be a medieval character and have battles and stuff with other people who are pretending to be different characters

dunk (pg. 32): If you've ever had a cookie with milk, you already know what this means. Sheesh.

duplicity (pg. 99): acting in two different ways to trick or cheat someone

dusky (pg. 81): that getting-dark time when day meets up with night. You might be able to see the Big Dipper.

dyed-in-the-wool (pg. 7): complete; through and through

dyslexic (pg. 99): when your brain tricks you by mixing up letters when you read and write

MY NEIGHBORHOOD

TO THE MALL

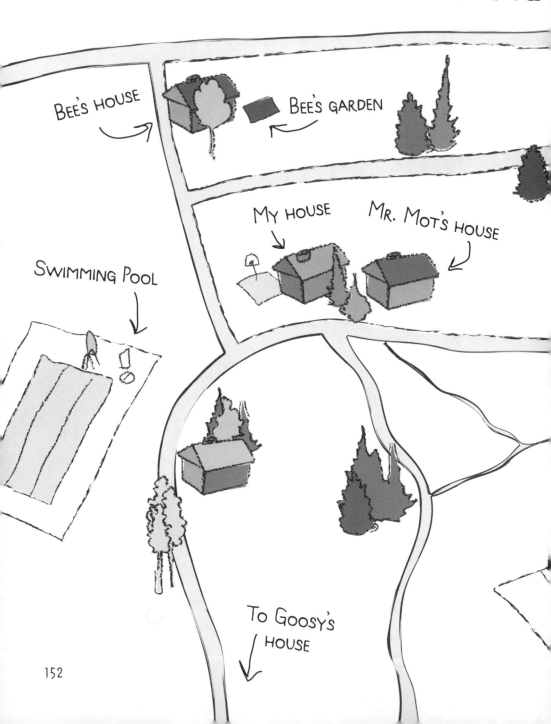

BEE'S HOUSE

BEE'S GARDEN

MY HOUSE

MR. MOT'S HOUSE

SWIMMING POOL

To Goosy's HOUSE

TOMMY GELLER'S HOUSE

DANA ELEMENTARY →

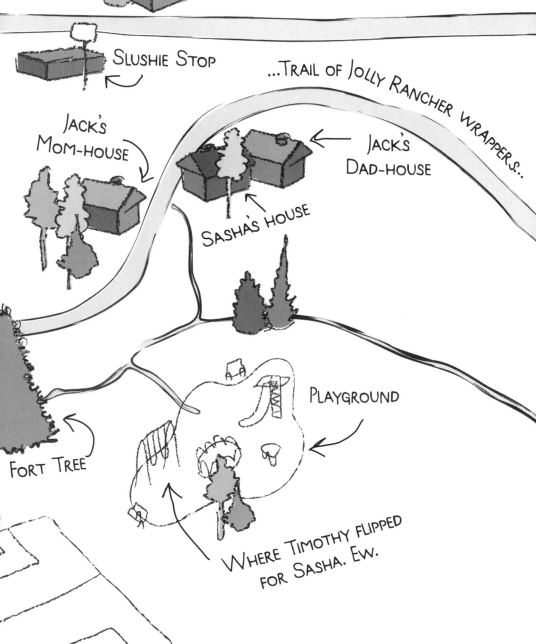
SLUSHIE STOP ←

...TRAIL OF JOLLY RANCHER WRAPPERS...

JACK'S MOM-HOUSE

JACK'S DAD-HOUSE ←

SASHA'S HOUSE

PLAYGROUND ←

FORT TREE ←

WHERE TIMOTHY FLIPPED FOR SASHA. EW.

ABOUT THE *award-winning* ALDO ZELNICK
COMIC NOVEL SERIES

The Aldo Zelnick comic novels are an alphabetical series for middle-grade readers aged 7-13. Rabid and reluctant readers alike enjoy the intelligent humor and drawings as well as the action-packed stories. They've been called vitamin-fortified *Wimpy Kids*.

NOW AVAILABLE!

160 pages | Hardcover
ISBN: 978-1-934649-04-6
$12.95

Part comic romps, part mysteries, and part sesquipedalian-fests (ask Mr. Mot), they're beloved by parents, teachers, and librarians as much as kids.

Artsy-Fartsy introduces ten-year-old Aldo, the star and narrator of the entire series, who lives with his family in Colorado. He's not athletic like his older brother, he's not a rock hound like his best friend, but he does like bacon. And when his artist grandmother, Goosy, gives him a sketchbook to "record all his artsy-fartsy ideas" during summer vacation, it turns out Aldo is a pretty good cartoonist.

In addition to an engaging cartoon story, each book in the series includes an illustrated glossary of fun and challenging words used throughout the book, such as *absurd, abominable*, and *audacious* in *Artsy-Fartsy* and *brazen, behemoth*, and *boisterous* in *Bogus*.

BOGUS
NOW AVAILABLE!

In this second book in the award-winning Aldo Zelnick comic novel series, Aldo and his best friend, Jack, find a diamond ring, which Aldo is sure is bogus—even though Jack—the rock hound!—believes it's real. Aldo loses then finds then loses the ring again, and bedlam ensues. Where will the ring turn up, and who will reap the rewards?

160 pages | Hardcover | ISBN 978-1-934649-06-0 | $12.95

CAHOOTS
NOW AVAILABLE!

Summer draws to a close, and the Zelnicks travel to the family farm in Minnesota for their vacation. But as Aldo fears, farm life isn't all it's cracked up to be. The rooster wakes him at dawn, the chores nearly do him in, and the cousins—identical twin pranksters—are in cahoots against him. All this without the comforts of TV or computer—because the Anderson farm is (gasp!) *technology-free.*

160 pages | Hardcover | ISBN 978-1-934649-08-4 | $12.95

EGGHEAD
COMING MAY 2012

It's October, and Aldo thinks he's Einstein. Gloating over his exemplary first-quarter grades and test scores, he even decides to dress as the iconic scientist for Halloween. But his bubble bursts when he realizes he's not excelling in one class, Español, and that the consequences may be more hurtful than a bad grade on a report card. Is Aldo's friendship with his bilingual best friend, Jack, at stake?

160 pages | Hardcover | ISBN 978-1-934649-17-6 | $12.95

BAILIWICK PRESS

www.bailiwickpress.com | www.aldozelnick.com

ACKNOWLEDGMENTS

"The course of true love never did run smooth."

— William Shakespeare, *A Midsummer Night's Dream*

Poor Aldo. Summer's over, and before he can even get his 5th-grade footing, he's felled by his first crush. Life—and art—are like that. Might as well just get in there and get messy, even if you sometimes end up stupefied at the result. Better to have been dumbstruck than never to have been struck at all.

We ourselves remain dumbstruck at the dogged support of Aldo's devotees. Thanks to: Cathy Bowles, teacher for the deaf at McGraw Elementary, who graciously donated her time and expertise; the dynamic team at Independent Publishers Group, without whose diligent distribution this series might have died on the vine; interns-with-derring-do Amy, Gretchen, Leon, and Reneé, who do everything we ask of them—and more; the Slow Sanders, for their doting discernment, or their discerning dotage (we're not sure which); and Launie, designer extraordinaire. We're grateful to our families for their faith in us and to Aldo's Angels for their divine intervention.

On to *Egghead*. Then...*Finicky*. You read it here first!

ALDO'S DECIDEDLY DIVINE ANGELS

Barbara Anderson

Carol & Wes Baker

Butch Byram

Annie Dahlquist

Michael & Pam Dobrowski

Leigh Waller Fitschen

Chris Goold

Sawyer & Fielding Gray (and Chris & Sarah)

Roy Griffin

Calvin Halvorson & Bennett Zent (and Chet)

Oliver Harrison (and Matthew & Erin)

Terry & Theresa Harrison

Richard & Peggy Hohm

Chris Hutchinson

Anne & Calvin Keasling

Vicki & Bill Krug

Cole, Grant, Iris, & Tutu Ludwin

Annette & Tom Lynch

Kristin & Henry Mouton

The Motz & Scripps Families (McCale, Alaina & Caden)

Jackie O'Hara & Erin Rogers

Betty Oceanak

Jackie Peterson

Ryan Petros

Terri & Dave Rosen

John Schiller & Suzanne Holm

Slow Sand Writers Society

Barb & Steve Spanjer

Dana Spanjer

Vince & Adrianne Tranchitella

Laura Welciek

Halo There! If you're an Aldo Zelnick fan, e-mail info@bailiwickpress.com and ask for details about becoming an Aldo's Angel. Angels receive special opportunities such as pre-publication discounts, free shipping, naming rights, and listing in the acknowledgments (especially fun for kids).

VISIT ALDOZELNICK.COM TO...

- join the Aldo Zelnick Fan Club!

- learn more about upcoming books in the series.

- hear how to pronounce the Gallery words.

- see the characters in full color and learn more about them.

- download coloring pages.

- suggest a word for an upcoming book.

- see Karla and Kendra's appearance schedule
  or invite them to your school, bookstore, or event.

- sign up for our e-mail list.

And don't forget to "Like" Aldo Zelnick on Facebook!

ABOUT THE AUTHOR

Karla Oceanak has been a voracious reader her whole life and a writer and editor for more than twenty years. She has also ghostwritten numerous self-help books. Karla loves doing school visits and speaking to groups about childhood literacy. She lives with her husband, Scott, and their three boys and a cat named Puck in a house strewn with Legos, ping-pong balls, Pokémon cards, video games, books, and dirty socks in Fort Collins, Colorado. This is her fourth novel.

ABOUT THE ILLUSTRATOR

Kendra Spanjer divides her time between being "a writer who illustrates" and "an illustrator who writes." She decided to cultivate her artistic side after discovering that the best part of chemistry class was entertaining her peers (and her professor) with "The Daily Chem Book" comic. Since then, her diverse body of work has appeared in a number of group and solo art shows, book covers, marketing materials, fundraising events, and public places. When she invents spare time for herself to fill, Kendra enjoys skiing, cycling, exploring, discovering new music, watching trains go by, decorating cakes with her sister, making faces in the mirror, and playing with her dog, Puck.

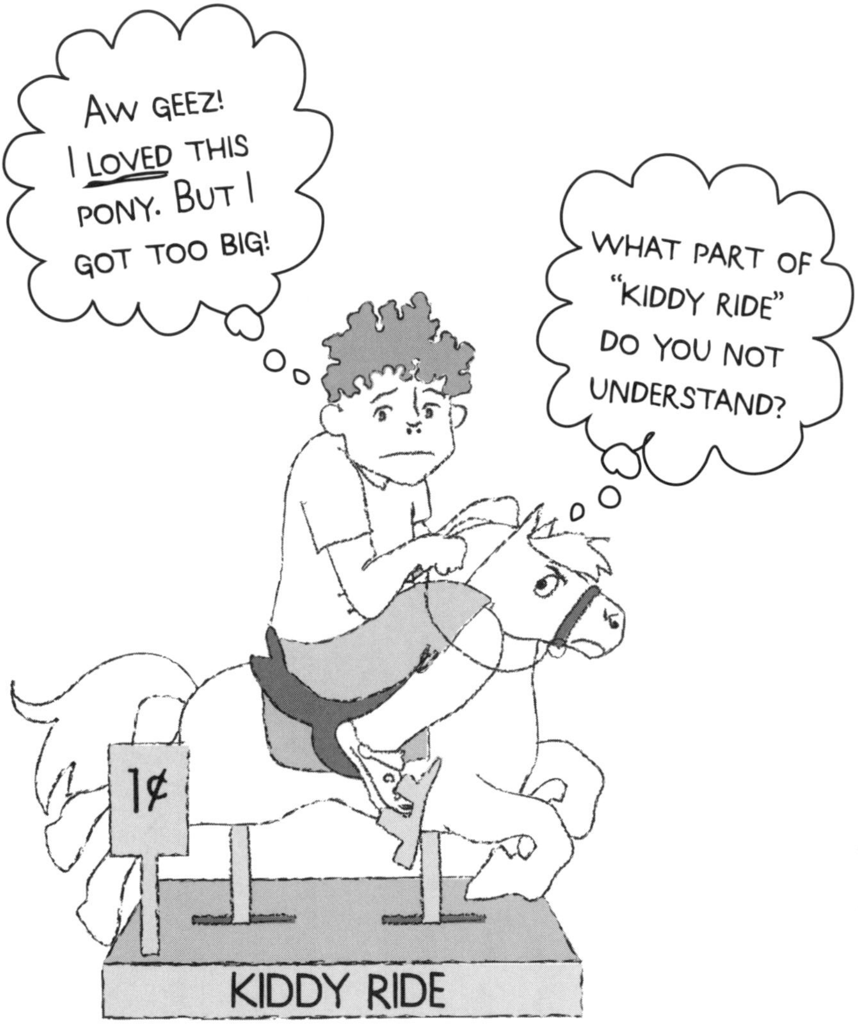

AW GEEZ! I LOVED THIS PONY. BUT I GOT TOO BIG!
WHAT PART OF "KIDDY RIDE" DO YOU NOT UNDERSTAND?
1¢
KIDDY RIDE